"We're not just losing the battle, we're losing the war."

Dr. Tang gave a frustrated wave. "I have more than six thousand dead in my own hospital. Men, women, children, babies. All die within a week . . . two weeks, with massive doses of Tricillin PDF. We haven't had *one* survivor. *Not one.* Do you know what that means?"

"I am well aware of the mortality rate." On the viewscreen, behind Tang, Dr. Crusher watched a dozen men dressed in white containment suits burst into the lobby from a side corridor. They began picking up the comatose patients and tossing them aboard a low, motorized cart—stacking them one on top of another like so much deadwood.

Bodies, Dr. Crusher thought with growing horror. *They haven't run out of beds, they've run out of slabs in the morgue.* A few limbs jutted out grotesquely from the growing pile on the cart. The toe on every left foot held an identification tag, she saw now. *They're all dead. Not just dozens, but hundreds of them.*

STAR TREK
THE NEXT GENERATION®

DOUBLE HELIX

BOOK ONE OF SIX

INFECTION

JOHN GREGORY BETANCOURT

Double Helix Concept by John J. Ordover and Michael Jan Friedman

POCKET BOOKS
New York   London   Toronto   Sydney   Tokyo   Singapore

An *Original* Publication of POCKET BOOKS

POCKET BOOKS, a division of Simon & Schuster Inc.
1230 Avenue of the Americas, New York, NY 10020

This book is published by Pocket Books, a division of Simon & Schuster Inc., under exclusive license from Paramount Pictures.

ISBN: 0-671-03255-0

First Pocket Books printing June 1999

10 9 8 7 6 5 4 3 2 1

POCKET and colophon are registered trademarks of Simon & Schuster Inc.

Printed in the U.S.A.

PART 1:

The Coming of the Plague

Prologue

WHEN HE REACHED the broad windows of his hotel room, Solomon paused in his security sweep. Fifty meters below, on the far side of the square, seethed an angry-looking mob of humans. He couldn't really make out faces in the growing twilight, but he knew their type. *Rabble-rousers. Troublemakers.* Fifth- and sixth-generation human settlers on Archaria III, gone back to a more primitive mindset. To a man they dressed in simple brown clothes—shirts, pants, and boots. All the men sported long bushy beards, shoulder-length hair, and smug attitudes of cultural and species superiority.

Solomon snorted. Superior? *Hardly.* Stubborn, closed-minded, and prejudiced against nonhumans . . . in a word, *fools*. He never had time for fools.

Still, he continued to watch. The mob continued to grow. He estimated their number now at more than a hundred. They milled about in the square, beyond the black marble fountains, and continued their angry posturing. As water jetted from the mouths of ten larger-than-life Earth lions, as gold and silver fish darted through the meter-deep series of oval pools, he heard their voices begin to chant: *"Veritas . . . Veritas . . . Veritas!"* loud enough to reach even where he stood.

He swung his gaze around the square, noting how dozens of shopkeepers—smooth-cheeked humans, gray-skinned Peladians, and even a couple of Ferengi—had already begun to trundle their wares inside to safety. Pottery, fruits, souvenirs, it didn't matter what they sold—they weren't taking chances. Solomon chuckled. They could read the signs as clearly as he. Another riot was brewing. As he watched, durasteel shutters snapped shut one by one across the stores' entrances and windows. He could imagine the merchants inside busily throwing bolts, latching latches, and retreating to the safest parts of their buildings. *Poor paranoid fools,* he thought. *Race riots are the least of your worries.* From the look of things, in five minutes every building facing the square would be locked up tighter than a Romulan clam. Not that it would save any of them in the end.

Still more bearded men streamed into the square from the side streets. Solomon leaned forward, searching for a leader, but saw no sign of the elusive man called "Veritas." The chanting built to a crescendo.

Snorting derisively, Solomon took a step back. *I really don't have time for this nonsense,* he thought. It was too easy to get swept up in the excitement. *Business calls.*

"Computer, engage privacy mode. Black out the windows. Filter extraneous noises." Civil unrest always made money for someone. *But not me, not today.* He sighed with regret. After all, he had bigger projects to finish before he even *thought* about fun.

The windows' glass darkened to the color of charcoal, and the room grew hushed. Not even the ventilators made a sound. Raising his tricorder, Solomon continued his security sweep. Good—no unexpected EM readings, no bugs, no monitoring devices. Business as usual on Archaria III; no one suspected him of being anything more than another buyer for the Interstellar Corn and Grain Combine. ICGC always made a great cover on farming planets like this one. He smiled a bit wryly. All he'd had to do was flash his business ID at the front desk and the hotel had rolled out the red-carpet treatment, complete with complimentary fruit basket and bottle of wine from a local vineyard. Second-rate stuff, of course, and he hadn't touched it; the best wines always came from Mother Earth.

Crossing to the bed, he lifted a small silver suitcase and gripped the handle long enough for the smartlock to scan his DNA. When it beeped acceptance, he flipped open the latches without triggering the small explosive device embedded in the handle. In fifteen years of illegal activities, he had never once lost his equipment . . . but the Orion Syndicate never believed in taking changes. And all due precautions were necessary on this particular job. The client had paid extra for them.

Nestled inside the case lay the pieces of a narrow-beam long-range subspace transmitter. He assembled it deftly, then used the tricorder to aim the short conelike antenna to the proper coordinates, about 20 degrees up and toward the square.

When he activated the device, a flickering holographic image filled the air before him: burning red eyes, a shock of long white hair, skin the color of milk: the General. *I hate this part.* Solomon blinked, but the General's features had already begun to change, thanks to the security scrambler: now the General had the prominent nose, black hair with blue highlights, and upswept eyebrows of a Vulcan. It would be this way throughout their whole conversation, as the scrambler shifted the General's features from one race to another. Solomon found it strangely disconcerting. *There's nothing like face-to-face meetings.* Next client. . . .

"Report!" the General barked, voice flat and artificial, revealing nothing about his species. Undoubtedly it had been so crunched and mangled by computers on his end that no trace of the original spoken words remained.

"Stage One has begun," Solomon said matter-of-factly. *Keep the client happy, the first rule of any service industry, even terrorism.* "All ten bombs are in place. The plague virus will be released per your timetable."

"Acceptable." The General nodded, the deep red waddles under his chin shaking to match his three antennae. He began to grow horns and ivory-colored tusks. "I will transmit the second third of your payment to your accounts on Ferenginar. The final installment will follow successful completion of this phase of the plan."

Solomon licked his lips. "General . . ."

"Speak."

"The vaccine—you're sure it will work?" If he was going to expose himself to some new genetically enhanced plague, he wanted every assurance that it wouldn't kill him.

"Yes."

"The Orion Syndicate does not tolerate damage to its membership," he added pointedly.

"I would not risk wasting talent such as yours. I will need it again." The General waved a puckered yellow tentacle as his gray-green face grew the cheek gills of an Eshashu. Then, with a brusqueness that matched his suddenly Klingon features, he severed the connection.

Solomon sat on the bed and chewed his lip for a second. He felt sweat trickling down his sides and back. Waiting always made his stomach churn. He felt control begin to slip away. It was one thing to belong to the Orion Syndicate, the most successful criminal organization in the Alpha Quadrant. Extortion, arson, blackmail, and even murder had long been a part of his life. But it was quite another thing to take a freelance job planting exotic diseases in unknown aliens and then sit calmly and wait for a virus to strike.

What if the cure didn't work? What if he *wasn't* immune? What if—

He drew a deep breath and forced himself to relax. *Steady, steady. No need to panic. I'm safe. Probably the safest man on the planet.* He didn't like invisible dangers, but at least he had been inoculated against them. *The Archarians must have done something to earn this strong a reaction from the General,* he thought grimly. *Poor bastards.* Then he forced such thoughts from his mind. He couldn't allow himself to start to feel sympathy.

Business was business, after all, and he was getting paid more than amply. Even after the Syndicate took its cut, he'd be well ahead for the quarter. Risa was getting boring; perhaps a well-earned vacation on Lomax or Gentree or one of the other up-and-coming pleasure worlds would soothe his nerves.

He glanced at the chronometer on the tricorder, still counting down to the carefully timed release of the plague. Just a few ticks more. . . .

"Nothing personal," he murmured to the million-odd humans and Peladians on the planet as the counter reached zero. He felt his heart skip as the moment came and passed, but he heard no sounds, no thunderous explosions, no vast collection of voices raised in cries of pain or sorrow or anguish as the invisible virus entered the planetary atmosphere. In his mind's eye, he saw it riding into the city on soft breezes, drifting like a fine mist through every street, into every home and business, into every set of lungs.

"Poor bastards," he whispered again. What *had* they done to the General?

Calmly he began to pack up the transmitter. Now, to see to the final part of the plans . . . he had to monitor how quickly the disease spread—and how quickly planetary authorities and the Federation dealt with it.

Let it be fast, he thought.

Chapter One

Stardate: 41211.0 Captain's Log, Supplemental

The *Enterprise* continues on its mission to
Archaria III, a planet jointly colonized by humans
and Peladians. A new disease has cropped up,
terrifying the inhabitants. So far, more than five
thousand cases have been confirmed.

The only drug at all effective in treating this
disease is a rare compound called Tricillin PDF,
which seems to prolong life, though only for a
week at most. The *Enterprise* will deliver a supply
of the drug, quarantine the planet, then stay to
oversee research into finding a cure.

"—AND RENDER WHATEVER AID the Archarians re-
quire until the emergency is over," Captain Picard
said, leaning forward at the conference table and
gazing at each of his senior staff in turn.

William Riker, Geordi La Forge, and Worf
looked uncomfortable at the mention of the plague,

and he didn't blame them; he had always felt ill at ease when faced with intangible dangers. Deanna Troi looked deeply concerned, and Dr. Crusher looked . . . intrigued? *She has dealt with plagues before,* Picard reminded himself. *She knows how to contain them.*

The persistent low rumble of a starship at maximum warp filled the room. None of his crew spoke. *They feel the tension building already,* he thought.

"Captain," Dr. Crusher finally said, "I may have to bring samples of this virus aboard the *Enterprise* for study, and perhaps a few patients."

"Understood, Doctor. So long as all necessary security precautions are maintained, I see no problem. In the meantime"—he slid a data padd across the conference table to her—"the doctors of Archo City Hospital have prepared a full report, which you may find useful."

"Thank you." She pulled the padd in front of herself and began skimming the opening remarks.

"Something else is troubling you, sir," Deanna Troi said softly.

Picard hesitated, then gave a curt nod. Best to get it out in the open. "What disturbs me most is the thought that this whole problem may be of our own manufacture . . . a biological weapon."

"Impossible—how could that be?" Riker said, shaking his head dismissively. "Legalities aside, it's against everything the Federation stands for!"

"We do have treaties with most sentient races which prevent the development and use of biological weapons," Data said. "With all due respect, sir, the deployment of a genetically designed plague on a remote agricultural world such as Archaria III seems highly unlikely."

"Not necessarily," Picard said. He cleared his throat. "Archaria III is in many ways a throwback to human civilization two or three hundred years ago. It was settled by religious zealots early in the twenty-second century, and although they have largely come into the Federation's fold, old prejudices and resentments still bubble to the surface from time to time." The room was quiet for a moment while Picard allowed his point to sink in.

Riker finally broke the silence. "Sir, if I may ask, what is it that leads you to conclude this disease is a weapon?"

"Might be a weapon, Number One. A radical political group called the Purity League claims the plague is an act of God against 'blasphemous unnatural unions.' "

Riker gave him a blank stare. "Sir?"

Picard cleared his throat. *How to phrase this delicately.* He said, "The Purity League is opposed to interspecies mating—'mixers' as they call such people."

Again the rumble of the ship's engines filled the room. *They can't believe it, either,* he thought. *Humanity is supposed to be beyond such prejudices.*

He noticed that Deanna Troi, half human and half Betazoid herself, hid her inner feelings behind a mask of professional calm. He would have given a lot to know her true reaction. Undoubtedly she was even more shocked and horrified than he had been.

To think that some humans are still capable of such petty resentments. . . .

He forced himself back to the problem at hand. "Mixers—or anyone else suspected of adulterating the purity of the human race—are treated as second-class citizens in many places on Archaria III," he continued. "Officially such prejudices are prohibited, of course, but in the backwater towns discrimination apparently still runs rampant. Only in the half-dozen large cities do humans and Peladians work and live together with something approaching harmony. In the country, things have apparently become so bad that most full-blooded Peladians now live in isolated enclaves surrounded by their own kind."

Riker said, "That sounds like a ghetto system."

"It is. Those of mixed heritage are even less fortunate, since they belong fully to neither the human nor the Peladian world. They were relocating to the cities in record numbers—until the plague struck. Now they're fleeing into the countryside once more, living like vagabonds in tent camps." Picard looked down at his clenched, interlaced fingers resting uneasily on the table. He didn't bother to feign relaxation. Sometimes it was good for the crew to see him share their anger.

Deanna Troi asked, "How many people of mixed blood are on the planet?"

"Nobody is quite sure. Estimates range from between 150,000 and 200,000 people. Obviously, those mixers who most closely resemble humans hide the truth to avoid conflict with the Purity League."

Data said, "I am aware of the Purity League, sir. The Federation has monitored their activities for many years, but has deemed them a minor nuisance with little actual influence."

"Their influence is growing," Picard said firmly. The private reports he had read gave alarming statistics; according to confidential surveys, fully half of the planet's human population harbored feelings of support for the Purity League, though the League's actual membership numbers were open to conjecture. It was certainly in the tens of thousands if not the hundreds of thousands.

He went on. "The Purity League's leader, Father Veritas, is using the plague as a rallying point for anti-alien sentiment. Apparently Veritas is responsible for inciting dozens of race riots in the last few months. The whole planet is in turmoil. The non-human population—and especially the partly human population—is running scared. The plague's growth has only served to make the situation worse." *"Veritas," indeed,* he thought, grimacing. *If ever there was a misnomer. . . .*

"Sir," said Deanna Troi, "Archaria III has a long history of interspecies problems, including wars, assassinations, and racism. Its history is part of several planetary evolution courses at the Academy. I believe everyone here has studied it to some degree."

A general murmur of agreement came from the

rest of his senior staff. Picard found himself surprised—it hadn't been part of the curriculum when he had studied at the Academy—but he was pleased. *They're keeping up with the times.*

"That is correct, sir," said Data. "It was settled in 2102 by a human sect of religious fundamentalists called the Brotherhood. Seven years later, these human settlers encountered Peladian settlers, who had colonized the planet almost simultaneously."

Picard had never seen a Peladian and knew little about them, beyond the fact that they were humanoid, militant about privacy, and generally considered pacifists . . . except when provoked.

Data went on, "After a series of small wars, as the two sides got to know each other, peaceful relations and coexistence began. According to the information I have accessed, with the increasing agricultural importance of Archaria III their differences were largely put aside, in favor of economic cooperation."

"That is the public story," Picard said. He folded his arms and frowned a bit. "There have always been tensions. Until Father Veritas and the Purity League burst onto the scene sixteen years ago, the planetary government managed to contain most of the problems before they escalated. Over the past few years, though, there has been an increase in terrorism on Archaria III aimed at Peladians, at humans who have married them, and especially at their children—all in the name of human racial purity. That's another reason why the Federation suspects the plague may be genetically engineered."

"I'm sorry, sir," Riker said. "I'm still not quite clear on what leads you to that conclusion."

Picard looked at Dr. Crusher. "Doctor?"

She looked up from scanning her report. "All the victims are of mixed genetic origins," she said flatly. "Not just human-Peladian, but several other genetic mixes have been affected as well. Human-Vulcan, human-Etrarian, and human-Bajoran crossbreeds are all reported susceptible to infection. Pure human and pure Peladian genetic stock appear to be immune. I would strongly suggest that no one of mixed heritage be allowed access to the planet."

The news cooled the room. Worf glared. Riker folded his arms and frowned pensively, though he kept glancing almost surreptitiously at Deanna Troi. And Deanna herself gave the slightest hiss of anger—she was the most threatened of those present, Picard knew, since she was half human and half Betazoid.

He looked pointedly in her direction. She returned his gaze, but whatever emotion had escaped her tight control had been suppressed once more behind that professional, clinical wall.

Counselor, counsel thyself, he thought.

Dr. Crusher continued, "The symptoms come on very quickly. Apparently the virus enters the mouth or nasal passages and primary multiplication occurs in lymphoid tissues. Small amounts of virus reach the blood and are carried to other sites in the reticuloendothelial system, where they multiply quickly. High fever and severe abdominal cramping are part of the first stage. Then small white fever blisters begin to cover the body, especially the face, neck, and under the arms. This second stage lasts from one to three days. Infected patients lapse into comas by this point—and it's probably just as well. The pain would be extreme as the muscle cramping worsens and fever blisters form in their mouths, throats, and lungs. Victims begin to suffocate. Next comes stage three, when blood begins to ooze from the gums, nose, and ears. Rapid cellular degeneration follows. Total systemic collapse is inevitable and occurs within a week of infection—often within three to four days."

Picard swallowed. Her matter-of-fact tone did not mitigate the gruesome truth about the disease. *Pain. Unconsciousness. Suffocation. Cellular degeneration. Death.* He had long harbored a secret fear of death by disease, by something slow and insidious worming its way through his body millimeter by millimeter. He liked enemies he could see, touch, and outsmart.

"*Could* such a disease be genetically engineered?" he asked her. No sense avoiding the inevitable question.

"Could someone create such a disease? Yes, I can think of half-a-dozen research labs capable of cobbling it together with a few months of hard work. I think the real question is, *did* someone. It's much too soon to say whether this disease has been genetically engineered. . . . It could just as easily be a virus which has mutated to attack some previously unknown weakness in the immune system of genetic crosses."

"How likely is *that?*" Riker asked her.

"I don't know." She hesitated. "I really can't comment until I get a sample of the virus and break it down with a microscanner."

"Our mission is to find out," Picard said. He looked at each of his senior staff in turn. "If this plague is a biological weapon, it must be contained, an antidote must be found, and the designers must be brought to justice before more damage can be done."

Dr. Crusher nodded. *Set her on course,* Picard thought, *and she'll work wonders.*

"I'll begin work with Archarian doctors at once," she said, "to try to find a cure. With so many people infected, that must be my first priority. I'll beam down with my team and begin work immediately."

"Agreed," said Picard. "Unless you have an objection, Doctor, I want an away team to beam down to investigate the Purity League. If they are responsible, they might already have a cure."

"That shouldn't be a problem, as long as no member of the away team is of mixed genetic heritage. And of course anyone who leaves must be fully decontaminated and possibly even quarantined before resuming normal duties aboard the *Enterprise.*"

"Very good."

"I'd like to head up that away team," Riker said.

"My thoughts exactly, Number One. Take two people with you. Use native costumes. This will be a strictly undercover mission. No one, not even the planetary governor, must know about it."

"Understood, sir," said Riker. "With your permission, I'll take Lieutenant Yar and Lieutenant Commander Data."

Picard nodded. "Very well, Number One. Any other questions?" He glanced around the table one last time, but nobody spoke. They knew their jobs, just as he knew he could depend on them.

Chapter Two

"Now entering orbit around Archaria III, Captain," Geordi La Forge reported from the helm, his voice rising above the electronic whirs, beeps, and chirps that signified that all systems were operating at full efficiency. When the young lieutenant glanced over his shoulder, Picard saw the bridge lights gleam across the metallic visor that covered his eyes.

"On the viewscreen." Picard leaned forward, anxious to see this troubled little world. "Standard orbit, Mr. La Forge."

"Aye, sir."

Archaria III appeared on the main viewscreen at the front of the bridge. It was a lush planet, half water and half land, with swirls of white clouds covering the northern hemisphere. The three main continents—colored in rich browns and greens, dotted with picturesque lakes and long flowing rivers—looked like a paradise to him. *And what have they done with it,* he thought bitterly. *They busy themselves squabbling over genetic purity.*

Sometimes he just wanted to grab planet-bound people by the scruff of the neck, drag them into orbit, and force them to gaze in wonder at the worlds they called home. If they could only see the hugeness of the universe, or realize just how insignificant they were in the greater cosmic vastness, it might well knock some sense into them.

The comm system beeped urgently. Beside Lieutenant La Forge, Ensign Cherbach touched his controls and reported, "We are being hailed, sir. Governor Sekk wishes to speak with you."

So it begins. With a mental sigh, Picard dragged himself back from his reverie. Standing, he pulled his uniform straighter and took a step forward. He wasn't looking forward to this conversation, but it had to be done.

"On screen," he said.

"Aye, sir."

The controls beeped softly in response, and the image of a balding, stocky man with a chest-length gray beard replaced the splendid view of the planet. Dark circles lined Governor Sekk's eyes, and deep worry lines creased his forehead. His ceremonial robes appeared rumpled and unkempt; several slight but noticeable food stains marked the front. *A good man pushed too hard,* was Picard's immediate reaction. *I don't think he's slept in days.* Clearly

Sekk took the plague, the Purity League, and all the attendant problems quite seriously.

As does Starfleet, Picard thought grimly. *As do we all.*

Even in the midst of crisis, protocol had to be observed. Picard inclined his head and got the niceties under way: "I am Captain Jean-Luc Picard of the *Enterprise.* Governor Sekk, I presume?"

"Yes, Captain." Sekk's voice was hoarse, Picard noticed. Too many orders over too many hours? Too many speeches to try to keep up morale? "Thank you for coming so quickly."

"Not at all, Governor. I understand the situation is still quite dire."

Sekk nodded. "Our morgues and hospitals are overflowing. There are fifteen thousand reported cases of the plague to date, with more being reported by the hour. Officially we now have more than ten thousand dead. Our cities are being abandoned. There are riots in the streets." His voice rose an octave. "We must have immediate help!"

"Of course, Governor. We have sufficient supplies of Tricillin PDF aboard to last your doctors for several weeks. The *Constitution* is bringing additional supplies and should arrive shortly. If your people will provide the necessary coordinates, our transporter rooms will begin beaming the drug down immediately."

"Of course, Captain." He motioned urgently to someone Picard couldn't see. "One of my aides will get the information for you."

"My ship's medical staff is standing by to work

with your doctors," Picard went on. "Any help they can provide will be given immediately. I believe Dr. Crusher, my chief medical officer, is already in contact with Dr. Tang at Archo City Hospital. I understand he is in charge of your efforts to find a cure."

"That's right, Tang is a good man. A very good man. Our best researcher."

Picard licked his lips. Now came the delicate part. The part he knew Sekk wouldn't like . . . and which he himself hated to have to do.

"Governor Sekk," he began, "as you can well imagine, the virulent nature of this disease has alarmed many of your neighboring star systems as well as Starfleet. All outbound ships have been ordered back to Archaria III. I am afraid I must place your planet under a quarantine, at least for the time being. No one may enter or leave."

Sekk seemed to shrink a little into himself. To an agricultural planet like Archaria III, quarantine would be viewed as nothing short of an economic death sentence; unless their grains and other food-stuffs were shipped out to market promptly, Archaria III's economy would begin to stagger and fail.

But the protests Picard expected never came. Governor Sekk only nodded wearily, as if he had been expecting it all along. "Very well, Captain. I will inform our spaceport at once. No more ships will be allowed to depart without Starfleet's approval."

Picard nodded. "Good." *Perhaps this won't be so difficult after all. If this is the level of cooperation I can expect, we should have the situation well in hand in just a few days.*

"Is there anything else you need?"

"I want to see a log of all outbound ships for the last three months, Governor, with flight plans. Plus passenger lists and complete cargo manifests. If any ships have to be chased down, we had best get started."

"Of course. The information is online with our spaceport's computers. I will make certain you have immediate access."

"Thank you." Picard hesitated a second. Sekk clearly *was* a good man, and his cooperation would undoubtedly come at a high personal price: after such a series of disasters—plague, planetary quarantine, economic ruin—he would stand little chance of being reelected planetary governor again. At least he could throw the man one little sop . . . something that might lead to a position within Starfleet's bureaucracy if Sekk followed up on it.

"I want you to know," Picard finally said, "that your assistance in this matter will not go unnoticed. I will personally see to it that your name is mentioned prominently in my reports to Starfleet."

Sekk nodded. "Thank you, Captain. But I would prefer your attentions go where they are most needed. Find a cure for the plague. Get the quarantine lifted. Help my people. That's all I really need." His smile was that of a kindly, benevolent ruler.

And a dozen red flags went up in Picard's mind. *He's hiding something.*

25

Picard returned that winning smile. "Understood, Governor. Thank you for your assistance. Picard out."

Returning to his command seat, he sat back and crossed his legs. *He's lying to me. Somehow, some way, he thinks he's pulled the wool over my eyes.*

He paused and thought, focusing not on the governor but on the people around him, trying to dredge some unvoiced suspicion from his subconscious. Officers hurried from station to station, scanning the planet and the rest of the system. The doors whooshed open as two more science officers came onto the bridge. The familiar chirps and beeps of the bridge filled his ears, along with the softer underlying bass vibration of a ship in orbit.

Picard retraced his conversation word by word, detail by detail. It *seemed* straightforward enough. Yet Sekk's all-too-convenient cooperation suddenly smelled wrong. *Why?*

The answer suddenly came to him: *So we won't suspect the data he provides.* Clearly the governor wanted to hide something. *But what?*

"Any thoughts, Number One?" he asked suddenly. He glanced at his second in command, still seated to his immediate right.

"I think he's playing us for fools, sir."

Picard covered his inner smile. *Riker will make a good captain someday. He's got the instincts for it.* "Fools, eh?" he said. "Would you care to elaborate?"

Riker hesitated. "I'm not sure, sir. I can't quite put my finger on it. . . ."

"Well, *I* can. I'll wager the governor sent his family off-planet in a private ship and doesn't want them sent back here. And I will be *very* surprised if we find a single reference to it in the spaceport's records."

Riker looked puzzled. "How did you know—"

"No career politician would surrender power so easily, Number One, and then refuse to take credit for it." He smiled a little grimly, thinking about the first time he had negotiated with the governor of a planet. He had been a lieutenant then, and Governor Silas Jones of the Rigel Colony had eaten him alive. "Sekk made one fatal mistake when he gave that stirring little speech about putting his people first."

Riker shook his head sadly. "Which is, of course, what a leader is supposed to do."

"Yes, but it was too easy, as if he would have turned things around so it looked like *he* gave us the records—in the best interest of his people, of course. Instead, he let me do all the work, then distanced himself from it. This way he hasn't lied or obstructed us in any way if the truth *does* come out."

"There's always one bad apple," Riker sighed. "Still, hopefully there are other people on this planet who can focus on more than their own interests."

It's nice to have an idealist for a first officer, Picard thought. *I know the Federation's philosophy will always be supported.*

"Sir," said La Forge, swiveling in his seat. "I have an idea of where we can find that extra ship."

"Oh?"

"Yes, sir."

Slowly Picard nodded. He liked initiative, and Geordi La Forge was another crewman who had the right instincts . . . and almost certainly could look forward to a long and distinguished career in Starfleet.

"Then it's your baby, Mr. La Forge," he said, settling back in his seat. "Proceed when ready."

"Thank you, sir."

Picard glanced at Riker again. "And now, Number One, don't you have an away mission to plan?"

Riker said, "It's well in hand, sir. Most of the Purity League's activities take place under the cover of darkness. We will be beaming down at dusk, and Lieutenant Yar is currently scouting the most likely spot to encounter them. I have already ordered native garb for the three of us. We will be ready on schedule."

"Excellent." Picard took a deep breath. *Like clockwork,* he thought with satisfaction. *A good ship runs like clockwork.*

An ensign appeared at his elbow holding a duty roster. After scanning the list of names, he signed off on it.

"Sir," said La Forge. "We have the spaceport's departure records now. Request permission to use the computer station in astrometrics for my research."

"Astrometrics?" Picard raised his eyebrows

slightly. It seemed an odd request. "Is there some reason you need access to interstellar charting, Mr. La Forge?"

"I have a theory about the governor's secret ship, sir. Call it . . . a hunch."

Picard thought it over a heartbeat. *Give him a chance. Let him prove himself.*

"Very well," he said. Hunches often had a grain of logic to them, even if the conscious mind couldn't always pin it down. "Carry on, Mr. La Forge."

"Thank you, sir." All business, the lieutenant rose and strode from the bridge with apparent confidence and determination. Ensign Charles Ehrhart moved forward to take La Forge's place at the navigator's station.

Like clockwork, Picard thought, leaning back and smiling to himself. *Excellent.*

Chapter Three

IT WASN'T DR. TANG'S APPEARANCE that alarmed Dr. Crusher—a week's growth of reddish-brown beard, pasty skin, puffy eyes, and wild unkempt red hair sometimes went with the territory when you where a doctor or a research scientist working in an emergency. Rather, it was what she could see behind him: hundreds of patients lying side by side on the floor in the hospital's lobby.

Plague victims, she knew without having to ask. *They must have run out of beds in the wards. This is the best they can do.*

It was a grim image, yet to her it painted a more accurate picture of the planet's situation than a host of dry reports and nameless, faceless statistics. Things had to be bad indeed if they had resorted to putting people on floors.

Her call to Dr. Tang had been routed to a public comm stand in the lobby of the Archo City Hospital. Tang had replied within five minutes of being paged. And when he answered, he cut through the usual niceties abruptly. "How soon can we get that Tricillin PDF beamed down here, Doctor?"

"The drugs are being prepared for transport now," she said. "The first fifty crates should reach your location in less than five minutes. If you can find a place to put them, that is," she added, peering over his shoulder. "You do look a little full."

Tang turned and called to someone Dr. Crusher couldn't see: "We need more room! The Tricillin PDF is here! . . . Right!" He turned back to her. "It will be taken care of. You can beam it down to these coordinates as soon as it's ready."

"Good." Dr. Crusher continued to stare at the hundreds of men and women and children beyond him. Something about them bothered her. They all lay curiously still despite being mashed in shoulder to shoulder and hip to hip. *Is this the comatose stage?* she wondered.

"Is there anything else you need?" She forced herself to focus on Dr. Tang. Brusque though he might be, he was still in charge of the hospital.

He snorted. "More doctors. A bigger hospital. A cure for the plague. Half a dozen tactical nuclear missiles lobbed at this city from orbit. Any combination of those will do."

Nuclear missiles? Was that an attempt at humor?

31

If so, she didn't find it particularly funny—and Tang didn't seem to be laughing, either.

"If you need more help, I will be glad to have some of my people beam down to assist—"

"No!" He almost screamed the word. "Keep your people off this planet! They'll be infected, too!"

"We have biofilters aboard—"

"Don't you understand? Didn't you read my report? They just *don't work!*" He sucked in a deep breath. "This virus isn't like anything you've seen before, Doctor. It . . . it's *smart.*"

She blinked. *Smart?* That didn't make any sense.

"Very well," she said coolly. "We can work from the *Enterprise* just as well, with your assistance."

He turned and paced away, then came back. His face was red, and he seemed to be struggling to keep his temper in check.

"Is something bothering you, Doctor?" she demanded, letting a professional mask hide her intense distaste for him. His appearance, his manner, his attitude—it all rubbed her the wrong way.

"Let me be blunt, Doctor," Tang finally said in a low voice. "We're not just losing the battle, we're losing the war. I have more than six thousand dead in my own hospital. Men, women, children, babies—" He gave a frustrated wave. "All die within a week . . . two weeks, with massive doses of Tricillin PDF. We haven't had *one* survivor. *Not one.* Do you know what that means?"

"I am well aware of the mortality rate." Beyond him, Dr. Crusher watched a dozen men dressed in white containment suits burst into the lobby from a side corridor. They began picking up the comatose patients and tossing them aboard a low motorized cart—stacking them one on top of another like so much deadwood.

Bodies, she thought with growing horror. *They haven't run out of beds, they've run out of slabs in the morgue.* A few limbs jutted out grotesquely from the growing pile on the cart. The big toe on every left foot held an identification tag, she saw now. *They're all dead. Not just dozens, but hundreds of them.*

As she gave an involuntary shiver, she met Dr. Tang's gaze again. He grinned at her now, widely, wolfishly, like a predator closing in on his next meal. *He's enjoying this,* she realized—and that horrified her almost as much as the bodies.

"Yes, Doctor," he said almost mockingly. "You start to understand the real situation now, don't you? It's not pleasant."

"How can you be so cold about it—"

He snapped back, "Don't judge us unless you've been in the same situation. You don't know how terrible it's been here. I—"

He paused and seemed to be trying to rein in his anger. Dr. Crusher didn't know what to say. She hadn't been in a situation like this before—and she hoped she never would be again.

In a calmer voice, Tang went on: "I know it's not a pretty little sickbay like you have aboard the *Enterprise,* but as you can see, we have room for that Tricillin now. Please get it down here as soon as possible, Doctor. We still have three thousand living patients who need it."

Dr. Crusher swallowed. "Immediately."

As a doctor, she had seen death many times and in many ways over the years, but even so, the cold unfeeling way these people were being tossed about still went against every grain of her moral and medical principles. She believed a certain dignity ought to come with death. The men in contamination suits might have been janitors cleaning up after a party instead of medical caregivers.

And Tang's rictus grin bothered her. Maybe it covered up a terrified interior, or maybe he had been pushed to the breaking point and beyond by the horrible tragedy unfolding around him, but she couldn't help how she felt.

He hasn't just lost his healing touch, he's lost his ability to feel empathy. He isn't a doctor, he's a . . . a body processor. The thought left her cold. *No matter how bad things get, I won't let it happen to me.*

"—and here is the access code for our medical computer's database," Dr. Tang was saying almost cheerfully, as though turning over the keys to a beach house. "You're going to need it." He entered it into the comm unit, and Dr. Crusher recorded it more by reflex than conscious thought. "It contains every scrap of information we have been able to gather about the virus. Precious little good it's done us. Thankfully, though, it's your problem now. *Starfleet's* problem, I mean. Good luck."

"Wait!" she said as he started to end the transmission. *That's it? He's just going to abandon me to my research? What kind of a madman is he?*

"What is it, Doctor?"

"I will begin reviewing your data at once." She swallowed at the lump in her throat. "In the meantime, I need a vial of contaminated blood beamed up. After that, I'll need a patient in the earliest stages of the disease."

Tang's eyes narrowed only the slightest bit. "I do not recommend that, Doctor," he said bluntly.

"Why not?" she demanded.

"The plague leaps through biofilters like they weren't there. For the first week, we kept them up around our quarantine wards, but it didn't help. Nothing stopped it."

"That's impossible," she said. "Nothing as big as a virus can get through a biofilter."

He shrugged. "Maybe we made a mistake. Maybe the plague virus was already loose everywhere on the planet simultaneously. Or maybe it's just smarter than we are. I just *don't know* anymore." He ran one hand through his unruly red hair. "But I still wouldn't risk it. Not aboard a starship. If it gets loose in a confined space like that, with your ventilator systems—well, I wouldn't want to be part of your crew. You'll end up spending the rest of your lives quarantined down here with the rest of us."

"We have air purifiers—"

"Not good enough." He shook his head. "Not even *close* to good enough. Why don't you *listen?*"

She sucked in an angry breath. *Count to ten. He's not deliberately trying to provoke you. Count to ten, and don't forget to breathe.*

"What *do* you recommend, then?" she managed to say in something approaching her normal tone.

He leaned forward, his expression growing even more intent. "I don't think this plague *can* be cured." His voice lowered to a whisper, as though taking her into his confidence. "Archaria III has one of the finest hospital systems in the Federation. All our equipment is new and top-of-the-line. Maybe not as good as you have aboard the *Enterprise,* but damned close. We haven't found an answer, and I've had a hundred people working on it for the last three weeks. We're not *going* to find an answer, Doctor. This is *it* for us."

"I refuse to accept that," Dr. Crusher said. With such a negative attitude, no wonder his people hadn't made any progress. "In human history alone, people have claimed that everything from polio to AIDS to cancer to Stigman's disease wasn't curable, and each time we've beaten the odds. There's *always* an answer. We just have to find it."

Tang leaned forward. "You want to know what I *really* think, Doctor? Do you want the best advice I can give?"

"Yes."

"Archaria III *must* be completely and forever isolated to keep the plague from spreading. Quarantine the planet, yes, that's a start. Post guards in orbit. Hell, *mine* the whole system! Shoot down any ship that tries to enter or leave. Cut us off from the galaxy, and never let anyone set foot here again! And pray—just pray—that the virus didn't jump planet with any of the dozens of starships that have already left."

Starships have been leaving? she thought with alarm. *Are they crazy?* Well, Jean-Luc would have to put a stop to that. She'd let him know as soon as she finished her conference with Dr. Tang.

"We *will* contain the plague," she said in her most reassuring tone. "This isn't the first disease Starfleet has faced, and it won't be the last."

Tang shook his head sadly. "Smug, arrogant Starfleet—you people always know better than the experts. Listen to me. This is the worst disease humanity has ever faced. It's airborne. There are *no survivors*. It kills everyone it infects. If it ever mutates . . . if it ever attacks nonmixers . . . Archaria will be a graveyard planet within a month."

Dr. Crusher swallowed again. *Some bedside manner.* Tang certainly wasn't pulling his punches.

"I must reserve judgment until I've had a chance to study your reports," she said flatly. "Have that blood sample prepared for transport. I'll let you know when I'm ready for a patient."

"Very well." He gave her a hopeless shrug. "It's your funeral. And others'. Check the video I sent. Tang out."

Taking a deep breath, Dr. Crusher sat back in her chair and chewed her lip thoughtfully. Around her, nurses and doctors bustled about their duties, setting up equipment, tending to a sprained ankle or a burned arm, conducting the routine physical exams that Starfleet required of every crew member.

Dr. Crusher ordered the computer to begin displaying the visual record Dr. Tang had sent. It showed a ten-year-old girl lying next to an older woman who, from the way she reached out to the little girl despite her own horrifying condition, could only have been her mother. They were dressed only in thin white smocks, although profuse sweating had turned the young girl's smock almost transparent and her devastated body showed through clearly. A cure would be found, and Crusher knew it, but it would come too late for this child and her mother. She had not even begun her work, but already Crusher felt that she had failed.

It can't be that bad. Nothing is ever hopeless. We will find a cure. She had to believe in herself and her people. How could she go on with her work if she didn't think they would succeed?

For a second, she thought about calling off the away team's trip to the planet. But no, she knew with 100 percent certainty that the *Enterprise*'s biofilters could remove anything as large as a virus, despite Dr. Tang's histrionics. He had made a mistake somewhere. *It's a scientific fact. Nothing as large as a virus can make it through unless we want it to.* Commander Riker's mission could prove the key to unraveling this whole medical mystery and finding a cure.

She tapped her combadge. "Crusher to Picard."
One last duty to attend to.

"Picard here," he answered immediately.

"Captain, Dr. Tang informs me that starships
have been leaving the planet since the plague broke
out."

"I am aware of it, Doctor. We are using their
flight plans to track them and order them back
here."

"Good. Thank you. Crusher out."

Reassured, she accessed the Archo City Hospital's computer, tapped in the access codes Tang had
given her, and found herself in the records
section . . . looking at thousands upon thousands
of recent files, all marked "Deceased."

On a sudden hunch, she called up Tang's personal records. *I want to see how well you do your job,*
she thought. *Since you think you're so good—let's
see you prove it!*

To her surprise, Ian Tang, M.D., Ph.D, had
received dozens of awards, commendations, and
citations for a career filled with exemplary work,
community service, and medical leadership. Not
only was he the finest virologist on Archaria III, he
had headed up half-a-dozen ground-breaking stud-
ies on Plimpton's disease—including several she'd
read. His name hadn't registered at first, but now
she recognized it.

*According to this file, he's just a few ticks short of
sainthood,* she realized. *Maybe he isn't exaggerat-
ing after all.*

Brilliant researcher or not, the official records

seemed quite a contrast to the man with whom she had just spoken. If everyone from the planetary governor to Starfleet's Admiral Zedeker spoke so highly of Dr. Tang's abilities, what could make him so determinedly pessimistic? *It's almost as though he* wants *us to abandon the planet,* she thought grimly.

A horrible thought came to her. *Abandon it . . .* maybe that *was* the answer. After all the mixers had been killed off by the plague, why not use the plague as an excuse to cut ties with the Federation?

It might just work, she thought. *If he can persuade enough people that there will never be a cure, the Federation may well post a permanent quarantine around the planet. And then the Purity League would be free to take over and run things exactly as they want, with their humans-first philosophy, devil take the Peladians.*

She shivered. He was a virologist. He said they had state-of-the-art facilities. Could Tang be part of the Purity League? Could he have engineered the virus? What figures did Jean-Luc cite? Wasn't half the planet supposed to be part of or at least in support of the Purity League? Why not a doctor, too. Why not Tang? She shook her head violently, as if to toss away the very thought.

Just because I don't like him doesn't make him a killer, she told herself.

Despite all his dire warnings, Tang proved true to his word. Within ten minutes the transporter chief hailed Dr. Crusher on the comm system.

She tapped her badge. "Crusher here."

"O'Brien in Transport Room One, ma'am. I have a medical shipment for you from Dr. Tang at the Archo City Hospital. He told me to leave it in the transporter buffer until you had a secure facility to hold it."

Dr. Crusher heard a note of hesitation in the man's voice. He wasn't telling her everything.

"Is there something else?" she asked.

"Doctor . . . is this whatever-it-is safe? If you want, I can rig up a couple of extra biofilters and run it through them before we materialize it—"

"No! Don't filter it!" she cried. That was the sort of help she *didn't* need. She still remembered one overefficient medical student in her class who tried to cut corners by beaming medical specimens from the lab to his research station. The biofilters had automatically filtered out the contaminants he was supposed to study, leaving him with useless tissue samples.

"Yes, ma'am!" She heard him jump.

She sighed. *Tang really got to me. No need to take it out on O'Brien.*

"I'm sorry," she said. "I didn't mean to snap at you, O'Brien. Just hold everything in the transporter buffer for now. Make sure you disable the biofilters—these are medical specimens, and I need the contaminants. I'll have a secure containment field ready for you in about sixty seconds."

"Right, Doctor."

"Crusher out."

She stood. "Computer, create a level-one containment field half on top of workbench one. Make it half a meter square on all sides. Tie in with Transporter Room One. The medical samples presently in the transporter's buffer must materialize inside the containment field. Do not run any biofilters!" She wasn't taking any chances.

"Acknowledged," the computer said. A forcefield began to shimmer faintly around the workbench. Dr. Crusher knew it would flicker out of existence just long enough for her samples to beam in, then the computer would make sure nothing got in or out. *"Level-1 containment field has been activated."*

She tapped her badge. "Crusher to Transporter Chief O'Brien."

"O'Brien here," he responded instantly.

"We're ready. Energize."

Lights twinkled around the workbench, and as they faded, she saw the small rack of a dozen tiny vials. Dark blood filled each one.

Now, my good doctor, she thought, *let's take a look at this plague virus of yours.*

Chapter Four

GEORDI LA FORGE FOUND a skeleton crew on duty in Astrometrics: three young ensigns, all hard at work updating the ship's navigation logs and starcharts with new files uploaded from Starbase 40 the day before. All three snapped to attention as he strode in.

"At ease," he said. It was obvious they were fresh from the Academy, all spit-and-polish and ready to impress superior officers. "I'm just borrowing a computer console for a little while. Carry on with your work."

"Yes, sir," they all said, and they turned back to their tasks with noticeably stiffer spines.

Geordi knew they felt his presence keenly: they worked with more speed, precision, and more professional demeanors—and far less banter—

than was normal for ensigns. He chuckled a bit, thinking back to his own days as a raw ensign. It felt like an eternity ago . . . and a different lifetime.

As the ensigns worked, they began calling off the new charts smartly. *They're trying to impress me.* Every few seconds, when they thought he wasn't looking (of course through his visor he saw it all, down to the 3-centimeter-long string that had unraveled from Ensign Barran's left sleeve), they glanced in his direction to see if their attention to detail was being duly noted.

Geordi focused on his own work instead. *First things first. . . .* He manually logged into the spaceport's computer system, then ran a quick search through the list of ships that had departed from the Archo City Spaceport in the last thirty days. One hundred and seventy-four in all, he counted, according to official records. He matched ships to ID codes and came up with a mix of 62 freighters and 112 passenger ships. A quick cross-check with the *Enterprise*'s records showed all the freighters had already been contacted and were supposedly en route back to Archaria III. *Simple enough.* The Federation moved quickly when a plague threatened.

Several of the freighters had already landed at the Archo City spaceport. He chuckled a bit to himself when he checked their status: it seemed their crews refused to disembark. They preferred the sealed environment of a starship to the open— and possibly plague-infected—air of the planet.

Call it self-imposed quarantine, he thought. Even

so, it wouldn't be good enough for Starfleet. The crews of those freighters wouldn't be leaving anytime soon, not until someone found a cure.

He moved on to the passenger ships. All ran commercially between Archaria III and a dozen nearby systems. And, as expected, all 112 had already been turned back to port here. Sixty-two had already landed again, and of those it appeared that most had also chosen to keep their hatches sealed. *More quarantines. And good luck to them.*

All right, the official ships were accounted for. Now came the fun part.

"Computer," he said. "Access service records at Archo City Spaceport."

"Accessing," the computer said. *"Ready."*

"How many starships have been serviced for departure at the Archo City spaceport within the last thirty days?"

"Two hundred and sixty-three," the computer replied.

He gave a low whistle. So many? He now had eighty-nine starships unaccounted for. Obviously quite a few must never have left the spaceport—once the quarantine order came down, they would have been stuck in their berths.

"List all the starships alphabetically and state their present location."

"The Alpha Queen, *en route back to Archaria III. The* Aspen, *parked in Berth 669-B. The* Belgrade, *parked in Berth 205-A. The* Brillman's Dream, *en route back to Archaria III—"*

The computer droned on through the names.

Geordi listened with interest until they reached *Zythal's Revenge,* a Klingon freighter.

"End of list," the computer reported.

Geordi frowned. Nothing seemed out of the ordinary. And yet, one ship had to be missing, if the captain's theory were right. *And I know it is,* he thought.

Where would you hide a starship? *Out in the open. You just change the computer records.* If the Archo City spaceport's records listed a ship as parked in its berth, the spaceport computer would perpetuate the lie when accessed by the *Enterprise*'s computer. It was a simple rule as old as computer programming itself, best known as GIGO: garbage in/garbage out. If you fed a computer faulty information, you got faulty information out.

Well, you might fool a computer, but you couldn't fool a security camera. At least not as easily.

"Computer," he said. "Access security cameras at the Archo City Spaceport. List all ships presently berthed there, and show me a current security camera image of each one. Begin alphabetically."

"The Aspen, *parked in Berth 669-B. The* Belgrade, *parked in Berth 205-A—"*

Within sixty seconds, he found the missing starship: a small five-passenger planet-hopper called the *Event Horizon* had vanished from its berth without tipping off the spaceport computers. His smile grew to a wide grin.

"Got you!" he said.

"Sir?" called one of the ensigns.

"Nothing." He cleared his throat and tried to sound officious. "Carry on."

The *Event Horizon* was originally a Vulcan vessel, he saw: a tiny T'Poy-class starship, capable of warp 2. The *Enterprise*'s computer had a schematic of that model on file, so he accessed it and looked it over quickly to refresh his memory: yes, warp capabilities . . . five passengers . . . slow but reliable. It would be perfect for sneaking off-world.

He could think of half a dozen ways to get such a small starship off-planet without leaving a record or setting off the spaceport's alarm systems. Methods ranged from the heavy-handed (bribing a clerk at the spaceport to make fraudulent file entries) to the daring (chasing a larger ship as it lifted off, and hiding in the shadow of its propulsion wake).

The most likely seemed bribery . . . even though it left one or more witnesses in place. After all, what starship pilot would risk colliding with a larger vessel when a simple bribe or two would do the trick?

Still, he had a little more work to do, just to make sure he had the right vessel. He hadn't yet established a link from the *Event Horizon* to Governor Sekk.

"Computer," he said, "where and to whom is the *Event Horizon* registered?"

"Accessing. The Event Horizon *is registered on Parvo IV to the Clayton-Dvorak Consortium."*

Who? Geordi scratched his chin in puzzlement. *The Clayton-Dvorak Consortium? Must be a farm-*

ers' combine or some sort. Which meant Governor Sekk's family had hitched a ride with friends . . . or the Consortium might be a front of some kind for the governor. . . .

"Locate the offices of the Clayton-Dvorak Consortium," he told the computer.

"Records indicate that the Clayton-Dvorak Consortium is no longer in business on Archaria III."

"Then where are they?"

"No information is available."

Could he have made a mistake? He stared at the empty berth where the *Event Horizon* should have been. *Starships don't just vanish.*

Even though Vulcans weren't known for building flashy starships, he knew they produced this particular model for export. It could be outfitted so opulently that a Roman emperor would have felt at home inside. It would have been perfect for a governor. No, Sekk wasn't off the hook yet.

Hmm. I'll come back to it. Geordi copied the information on the *Event Horizon* to a separate file. Maybe inspiration would strike after he finished looking through the rest of the records. First things first.

"Proceed with the display," he said. "Show me the next ship that's supposed to be in its berth."

And ten seconds later, he had his second match: the *Falcon's Talon,* a Klingon freighter that was supposed to be picking up five hundred metric tons of grain. And twenty seconds after that, the *Halibut* turned up gone. Followed shortly by its sister ship, the *Hemlock,* then the *Langley,* the *Middlemarch,* the *Nesfa*, the *Prushnikov*, and ten more. Geordi logged their absences with growing disbelief. All told, sixteen ships had disappeared from their berths in the spaceport without leaving any records of their departure.

Captain Picard is not *going to be happy*, he thought. *At least, not with the governor or the spaceport's security officers.*

He began checking ship's registries. As the captain had anticipated, one had been registered in the name of Armand Sekk, the planetary governor: the *Nesfa*.

"Computer," Geordi said, "locate Captain Picard."

"Captain Picard is in his ready room."

Geordi loaded the information on the missing ships into a data padd, then rose and hurried toward the turbolift. He had quite a report to make . . . and unless he'd missed his guess, the fireworks were just about to begin.

Chapter Five

DR. CRUSHER RAISED her medical tricorder and took a quick scan of the vials of contaminated blood: yes, her plague specimens had arrived intact; that overeager transporter chief hadn't run them through the biofilter after all.

According to the readings, nothing—literal vacuum—now surrounded the rack within the containment field. Not a single stray oxygen or hydrogen atom, let alone any virulent microbes, existed outside of the vials. She planned on there being no chance of the virus being let loose on the *Enterprise.*

"Computer, shut down forcefield," she said. It collapsed with the inevitable sharp snap of air rushing in to fill a suddenly exposed void. "Activate the microscanner."

"Microscanner ready."

Dr. Crusher picked up the first vial and swirled it slowly. Inside, the tainted blood looked just the same as any other human's. *If only it were so simple,* she thought with a sigh. *If only we could see the virus with our naked eyes, it would be so much easier to defend against it.*

She slipped the vial into the microscanner. The machine made the faintest of whirring sounds as— all within its self-contained unit—it unsealed the vial, loaded a sample, and initialized its diagnostic computer.

"Show display."

"Display activated."

A holographic image of the sample appeared in front of her: a three-dimensional pink field swarming with microscopic activity. Normal red and white blood cells swirled in and out of view, followed by oddly shaped T-cells, Y-cells, J-cells, and all the other components of a half-human, half-Peladian blood sample. Fortunately, Dr. Tang's notes had prepared her as to what she would find in a "normal" mixer's blood.

There! she spotted the invading virus . . . an almost triangular gray puff, with dozens of tiny tendrils radiating from its core. It really did look like the Rhulian flu, she thought.

The microscanner focused in on it at once, expanding until the virus took up the whole projection.

"Virus found."

"Begin comprehensive analysis of virus sample," she said. "Start with TXA sequencing and protein-strand breakdown. I want a level-one analysis."

The computer responded: *"A level-one analysis will take approximately fifty-two minutes."*

"Proceed. Display tests as they are completed."

"Working."

The image of the virus split down the middle as the microscanner began to take it apart protein strand by protein strand. Of course Dr. Tang had already run this test, but true research always began with an independent analysis.

Dr. Crusher watched the microscanner work for a moment, then stood and stretched. *This is going to be a two-cup job,* she thought. She headed for the replicator unit and the tea Jean-Luc Picard had recently introduced her to, Double Bergamot Earl Grey.

Captain Jean-Luc Picard kept his face neutral while Lieutenant La Forge made his report. Inside, though, he seethed with anger. *Sixteen missing ships! This is an outrage—how could Sekk possibly think he could get away with it?*

It certainly warranted an immediate call to the governor . . . and the immediate dispatch of alerts to every planet and starship in the sector. Those ships would be sent back to Archaria III on the double, and under armed escort, or they would face the consequences of defying Federation law.

"Very good, Mr. La Forge," he said. "Well done."

"Thank you, sir." La Forge handed him the data padd, and Picard glanced over the names of the ships once more. *Sixteen!* He couldn't believe it.

After downloading the information into his private log, he handed the data padd back. "Post an immediate alert to all ships, planets, and starbases in the sector. Anyone spotting one of these ships is to report it at once—and avoid making direct contact. The nearest Federation ship will provide armed escort back here. If they ran once, we don't want to risk them running again."

"Understood, sir." La Forge turned smartly and hurried from the ready room.

Picard leaned back and rubbed his eyes with the palms of his hands for a second. He had no choice but to make a second call to the governor, and he looked forward to this one even less than the first. For a second he wished for the authority to remove Sekk from his elected job, but then he thought better of it. He didn't want to bog himself down with the onerous administrative chores of running a planet if he could possibly avoid it. Bad as he might be, Sekk at least understood the job.

"Computer," he said. "Get me Governor Sekk."

The computer bleeped, and a second later an even more harried-looking Governor Sekk appeared on the smaller monitor on the captain's desk.

Sekk gave a cursory nod, then asked, "What is the problem, Captain—this really isn't a good time. I am in the middle of a dozen crises here—"

"I'm afraid you're going to have to make time, Governor. Have you ever heard of a ship called—" he consulted the list. "The *Nesfa?*"

Sekk paled suddenly. He turned and bellowed, "Clear the room!" to his assistants. "I need to talk to Captain Picard alone! *Out!* All of you!"

They scrambled for the doors. The moment he was alone, Sekk turned back to the comm. Picard saw new lines of worry crease the man's face.

"If I claimed I hadn't heard of the *Nesfa,* it would be a lie. You know that. Let's not play games, Captain. You caught me; I confess. I need to know—is there something wrong with the *Nesfa?* It hasn't . . . met with an accident, has it?"

"Not that I know of, Governor. But I think it's time you told me the whole truth about what's going on here. I don't like being lied to—even if it's a lie of omission!"

Sekk sucked in a deep breath. "My wife and children are on board the *Nesfa.* My eldest son, Derek, took everyone off-planet the day the hospital reported the first plague cases. I wanted them safe. Is that a crime?"

"No, Governor. It's perfectly natural. Unfortunately, we're going to have to bring them back. This system is now under quarantine . . . and that applies to everyone, even your family."

"But you don't understand . . . my wife, Mira . . .

she's half Peladian. If she comes back here, it's a death sentence for her. And for our four innocent children, Derek, Robin, Eric, and Denny. Denny is only two, Captain. Bringing any of them back is nothing short of murder."

Picard swallowed. "Decisions like this one are never easy. But I can't make exceptions, even for you."

"I realize that, Captain. But you don't have to, at least not in this case. You see, they are still technically on Archaria III."

"Enough games, Governor. I need to know where they are. *Exactly* where."

Still Sekk hesitated. "You understand, of course, that I had to weigh my duties carefully. And this time I'm afraid my family won."

Picard frowned. Sekk certainly wasn't making this easy. "How do you know your family wasn't exposed to the plague?" he asked. "How do you know they aren't passing it on to others right now?"

"They left thirty-two days ago—on the day the first victims began flooding our hospitals, as I told you. Since the first symptoms appear within a few hours of exposure, and I talked to them not ten days ago, I know they're well." Sekk swallowed. "At least, I think so. I just haven't been able to raise them on the comm since then."

"Where are they?" he asked again.

"On Delos—our smallest moon. There's a research base there. It's been deserted for years. I don't think many people know about it any more . . . but the equipment is still functioning." He twisted his hands together. "I thought they would be safe there, Captain. And technically they *haven't* left Archaria III."

Picard frowned. A game of semantics . . . but true, in a manner of speaking. Starfleet classified moons as part of the planets they orbited.

"Governor . . . far be it from me to doubt your word, but I'm going to have to check your story. If your family *is* there, then we will be glad to render whatever assistance they may need, from repairing their comm systems to an emergency evacuation to the *Enterprise*. However, if they are *not* there . . ." He left the threat hanging.

"Understood, Captain. And if there *is* something wrong, I need to know immediately. I . . . I almost told you about them earlier. But I couldn't bring myself to do it. I hope you understand."

All too well. You didn't want to jeopardize your own position. Never mind that your family could be dead or dying and you wouldn't know about it.

Picard said: "I will keep you up to date. Next, I need you to look over this list of ships. What can you tell me about them?"

Picard transferred the whole list of missing ships to the comm unit. He knew Sekk would be seeing it on his end of the channel.

The governor read it over slowly, then shook his head. "I don't understand. What about them?"

"They are missing. Like the *Nesfa,* they have disappeared from their berths at *your* spaceport seemingly without a trace. I need to know what happened to them. Where did they go, Governor? How big *is* your family?"

Sekk bristled a little at that jab. "I don't know anything about these ships. But I *will* find out." From his tone and expression, Picard actually believed him this time. *His security system has as many holes as a sieve.*

He asked, "Is two hours sufficient time?"

"It should be." Sekk paused and licked his lips. "Captain . . . let me thank you in advance for not mentioning how my family left the planet to anyone else here. The situation is . . . *delicate* right now. Such news might well tip the scales toward the Purity League and chaos."

"I won't lie about it, Governor, and all the details *will* be in my report to Starfleet. But I have no intention of making any public proclamations, if that's any reassurance."

The new look on Sekk's face spoke more clearly than words: the governor was hardly satisfied. Even with the information buried in an official Starfleet report, dozens of eyes would see it on Archaria III. And some of those eyes undoubtedly would belong to the governor's political enemies, Picard knew.

I know how to play this game, too, Picard thought with a twinge of self-satisfaction. *You won't pull the wool over my eyes a second time and get away with it, Governor.*

"Thank you," Sekk finally said, sounding strangled.

"You're welcome, of course." Picard gave him the same warm smile he normally reserved for unsavory diplomatic functions. "Picard out."

The screen went blank. Taking a deep breath and dropping his phony expression, Picard rose and strode out onto the bridge again. The low rumble of the engines and the beeps and whirs of the controls proved a tonic for his nerves, and he let out his breath with a sigh, starting to relax again. La Forge had reclaimed the navigator's station and Riker had vanished . . . probably finalizing preparations for his away mission. *Like clockwork,* he thought. The mechanism of the ship continued to run without him.

Yet their problems had only just begun. *Fifteen more ships to find . . . and a moon base to uncover,* he thought. This job was not getting any easier.

"Mister Worf," he said, taking his command seat.

"Sir?" came the low Klingon growl.

"Please initiate surface scans of the planet's smaller moon, Delos. According to the governor, there is a small research base there. I want it found. There should be a starship and hopefully five life forms."

"Scanning . . . I have it, sir."

That was fast. "On screen."

The pock-marked face of the little moon appeared. Nestled within a large crater lay a complex of perhaps a dozen white-domed buildings, all interconnected by silver tubes—walkways of some sort, Picard assumed. Lights gleamed from all the windows. *At least they still have power.*

His gaze drifted to the base's landing pad—located on the far side of the crater and presently half masked in shadow. It contained not one, but three ships. It seemed the governor's family was entertaining at their private hideout, he thought. He narrowed his eyes. One ship had almost Klingon lines. Could it be one of the two missing Klingon freighters?

Klingons might well explain the silence, he thought. *If they decided to move in and take over, I can see them smashing all the communications equipment.*

Unfortunately, he could also see them killing everyone in sight if sufficiently provoked.

But we mustn't jump to conclusions, he thought. *Nothing is wrong until we prove it wrong.*

"Can you identify those ships?" he asked Worf.

"Not yet, sir. They do not respond to hails."

"How many life forms are on the base?"

"Sensors pick up thirty-six," Worf reported. He looked up. "Ten are Klingon!"

Picard nodded with satisfaction: it had to be the missing freighter. That meant one less ship to worry about. Possibly two, if the third ship proved to be one of the missing vessels.

"Hail the base. And hail those ships again."

". . . Still no response, sir."

Blast. Why did everyone on this wretched planet have to make things more difficult? Picard stood and began to pace, arms behind his back, thinking. *One starship isn't enough to police a whole planet. If only the* Constitution *were here, we could split up duties.*

"Sir," said La Forge. He had been adjusting the controls for the viewscreen. "I believe you should take a look at this."

Picard turned. Under extreme magnification, one of the windows of the research station looked into a room . . . and on the floor of that room lay a human body . . . a man. His face was turned away from the window, but Picard could just make out the edge of his beard. *Could that be Derek Sekk? Or is it someone else?* A dark liquid—it looked like blood—had pooled around the man.

That settled things. If violence had broken out on the research station, he had no choice but to investigate. More lives might be at stake.

"Mr. Worf, coordinate with Lieutenant Yar before she leaves for her away mission. I want a team assembled from available security officers." *Klingons are down there.* "You will lead them, Mr. Worf. Heavy weapons, full contamination suits, and all due caution. Please bear in mind that this is a fact-finding mission, not a military assault."

"Yes, sir!"

Picard thought he detected a note of near glee in Worf's voice.

"Remember," he went on, "we do not know the situation on that base. I don't want to start a firefight if we can avoid it. But if anyone there needs medical or other care, we must be prepared to provide it."

* * *

Two cups of tea would not be enough, Dr. Crusher thought. She drank; she paced; she fretted; she stared at the unfolding computer model of the virus, still being mapped out in all its minuscule glory.

The rest of the medical team began to gather around the workbench. They, too, stared at the display, mesmerized: the nurses, the doctors, and even the biologists currently aboard the *Enterprise* all came in to watch. She had alerted anyone who might have an insight into the origin, treatment, or cure for the virus.

The talk around her grew hushed and subdued. *They feel it, too,* she thought. *We have barely begun work on the virus, and already the strain shows. No wonder Dr. Tang is at the end of his mental rope.*

Still, it was hard to feel sorry for Tang. Under the worst circumstances, that's when a person's true spirit showed. *And here I am, calmly sipping my tea, waiting for the computer to beep and say my cake is ready for frosting.* Reminded of her drink, Dr. Crusher took another sip—*feh, getting cold.*

Her thoughts turned back to her conversation with Dr. Tang. *What if he's right and we can't find a cure? What about all those people dying down there?*

An old saying came to her: Time resolves all problems. *Not this problem,* she thought.

She drained her tea, rose, and got another cup. Five more minutes. A three–cup solution.

It seemed an eternity, but finally the microscanner finished and beeped. She jumped, startled, and spilled a few drops onto her knees. *I should have seen that coming,* she thought. A hush fell over the room.

"Analysis completed," the computer proclaimed.

"Display the report." She leaned forward. Everyone around her did, too. She felt them holding their collective breath, just as she held her own.

"Virus appears to be a previously unknown variation of Rhulian influenza." A model of the triangular virus appeared, turning slowly before them. The computer began its breakdown: *"This virus consists of a single molecule of RNA surrounded by a 27-mm-diameter protein capsid and a buoyant density in CsCl of 1.39 g/ml. This molecular breakdown shows 36 percent carbon atoms, 21 percent oxygen atoms, 20 percent hydrogen atoms, 17 percent—"*

"We already know that," Dr. Crusher muttered to herself. "We all know what Rhulian flu is made of!" More loudly, she added: "Show the protein and NXA strands. Compare and contrast to Rhulian flu, type one."

Twisted lines of interlocking RNA strands appeared before her, rotating slightly. The NXA sequences were almost identical . . . though she immediately spotted several differences in key strands, especially the T-cell inhibitors. And some of the strands just didn't seem to belong . . . as though they had mutated . . . *or been grafted on from some other virus,* she thought uneasily.

Assuming it's engineered, she thought, *whoever made it did a good job.*

She glanced at Ian McCloud, the ship's microbi-ologist. "What do you think?" she asked him.

He frowned. "I am a little disappointed," he said in his slightly lilting accent. "It would appear to be a fairly simple virus. The Rhulian flu NXA strands were catalogued thirty years ago—I see only a few minor differences." He pointed. "Here, here, and here. And—*hello!* What's this?"

"What?" Dr. Crusher demanded.

McCloud said, "Computer—stop the projec-tion. Turn it back three seconds. There, Doctor!" His finger jabbed at one NXA sequence. "Do you see it?"

Dr. Crusher leaned forward. She didn't see anything out of the ordinary. And then it all but leaped out at her . . . the virus had a strange little hook on the very end of one NXA protein strand . . . an extra NXA code. She felt a surge of excitement. She had never seen anything like it before on a virus. *This could be it! The key to the mystery!*

"Yes!" she breathed. "What *is* that?"

"If I recall the Rhulian flu correctly, it's attached to the NXA strand that controls the shape of the virus." McCloud frowned. "I would need to look it up to make certain."

"You're right," Dr. Crusher said, disappointed. *I should know not to get my hopes up. It's too soon in our research.* "I remember it, too."

"Oddly enough, despite that change, the virus looks the same . . . exactly like type-one Rhulian flu. I find that odd. *Very* odd. A mutation large enough to show up in the NXA strands should be visible."

"That's right." Dr. Crusher sighed. It was puzzling. A dead end? Still, anything unusual gave them a starting point.

To the computer, she said: "Run a full development sequence on NXA protein strand—what's its designation?"

"445-J3," McCloud said.

"445-J3. *Build it!*"

"Working," the computer said. The display went blank, and then, in extreme closeup, it began to assemble one of the tendrils. The hook appeared to add a slight texture to the underside, as far as Dr. Crusher could tell. A new genetic sensor of some kind? Something to detect a flaw in the cells of a person with mixed human-alien heritage?

The computer finished rendering segment 445-J3. The texture curved down, then up in a winding, almost snakelike pattern. She had never seen anything quite like it before.

A shudder went through her as a horrible inspiration struck. *It's not a random pattern.*

"Freeze image," she said. The computer diagram paused. The textured curves rolled gently down then up, a valley and a hill . . . or a letter lying on its side?

She said, "Rotate ninety degrees counterclockwise."

The tendril turned slowly. The curves suddenly

became the letter "S." No one could have mistaken it. The texture extended to the right after a slight separation . . . another letter? The initials of its designer, perhaps?

A hush fell over the room. *They see it, too,* she realized. *I'm not crazy.*

She brushed back her red hair with one hand. *One letter could easily be a fluke of nature,* she told herself. It proved nothing. *Unless . . .*

She didn't want to give the command. Its potential repercussions were too great. But it had to be given: "Pull back slowly."

More of the tendril began to appear. S—M—I—

People around her gasped. She felt her heart skip a beat. *A message. It's a message.*

Letters continued to appear: L—E—Y—O—

Dr. Crusher found herself mouthing the syllables.

U—A—R—E—D—E—A—D

Smile. You are dead.

It felt like a knife puncturing her stomach.

That's why it looked so much like Rhulian flu. It *was* Rhulian flu, but modified to carry out a very specific and a very deadly attack.

She exchanged a glance with Ian McCloud and found an expression of horror equal to her own on his face . . . and on the faces of everyone around them.

"The bastards . . ." Nurse Icolah breathed. "Those *bastards!*"

"Now we know what we're up against," Dr.

Crusher said flatly. "This is actually good news. If someone made this virus, we can unmake it."

Deep inside, she knew it was the merest accident that she had stumbled onto the message, one chance in a million. If Ian McCloud hadn't spotted the odd hook, if she hadn't sequenced it, if the shape hadn't struck her as odd—if any of a thousand variables hadn't happened to come together just right—the twisted conceit of whatever bioengineer was responsible for the plague never would have been uncovered.

She regarded the computer model thoughtfully. The letters had been programmed into the virus on a protein level. That took some doing. And she wasn't quite sure *how* it had been done.

At least I'll have something new to tell Dr. Tang now, she thought with a morbid mental grin. *And it's something sure to wipe that smug look off his face.*

The truth hadn't quite sunk in yet. *They left a message on the protein level.* Who would want to sign a genetically designed virus? *Someone vain. Someone smart. Someone crazy.*

As for who . . . Starfleet's research centers could do it. But they wouldn't. She racked her brain for other possibilities. Vulcans, of course . . . and certainly the Romulans and the Cardassians. But not the Klingons . . . they wouldn't bother, even if they understood the underlying technology. Klingon medicine had barely advanced beyond leeches, in her opinion. *And an attack on innocent half-breed humans would be incredibly dishonorable,* she reminded herself. No, it couldn't be the Klingons.

Who else? Perhaps half-a-dozen other races had the technology, from the Tholians to the Praxx.

But why bother? Why would *anyone* bother to create a virus that only attacked this specific genetic weakness, then let it loose on Archaria III?

The Purity League had a motive. After all, they had embraced the plague as an easy way to rid their planet of the "mixer influence." Why not push it a little farther? Why not *create* the plague to do the dirty work?

Smile. You are dead.

Much as she tried to deny it, those four words spoke volumes. They were written in standard English. *That means humans did it. Or at least one human.*

Dr. Tang? She didn't know. How many other brilliant virologists could there be on Archaria III? And yet without proof, she wouldn't dare accuse him. *So how do I get proof? Confront him? Beam down and ransack his office? Send in my spies?*

She stared at the virus. *Smile. You are dead.* The message had to be a private joke, since no one else could have been expected to find it. A mocking little tag line, petty as a schoolyard bully's taunting.

So much for the transcendent nature of man, she thought bitterly. Those four little words kicked the legs out from under her belief system. *We think we've come so far. And yet we are still capable of this.*

She stood. Her doctors and nurses all looked stunned. The biologists looked stricken. McCloud had gotten over his terror and now looked intrigued. Grudgingly, she admitted the person responsible for the virus showed some real creativity. *McCloud wants to know how they did it.*

And, she realized, *so do I.*

And, she realized, the signature gave her more hope. Anything one human could do another human could undo.

First things first, though. Rumors about the virus would sweep the ship if she didn't put a stop to them now.

"This message is hereby classified top secret," she said, looking from face to face. Her people began to nod; they understood. *Loose lips sink ships.* "I don't want a whisper of what we've found getting out to anyone," she said firmly. "We don't want to create a panic . . . or a war." The Peladians might well adopt a hard stance if they knew humans had created this plague.

Of course, they would find out eventually, but right now didn't seem like a particularly good time. *Their children are dying, too,* she thought. *It's easy to lose control when it's your loved ones whose lives hang in the balance.* She didn't know what she'd do if Wesley came down with a disease like this plague virus.

One person had to be informed immediately, however. Tapping her combadge, she said, "Crusher to Captain Picard."

"Picard here, Doctor," he answered.

"I . . . think you'd better come to sickbay. I have something for you to see."

"Doctor, I'm rather occupied right now—"

"Captain, *it's important.* I need you here *now.*" She had never used that tone with him before, her Voice of Authority—usually reserved for Wesley on his bad days. *Not that he has many of them anymore.*

Captain Picard seemed to pick up on the importance of her request. He sighed, but said, "On my way, Doctor."

Chapter Six

THE DOOR TO TASHA YAR'S CABIN whisked open at her command, and Worf poked his head inside. "Lieutenant?" he called.

"I said come in!" She was in the next room. "I'll be right there."

He stepped inside, already ill at ease. Though he had been raised among humans, he felt his Klingon heritage most keenly in one-on-one meetings and social situations. It happened more and more as he ran up against what he considered the "human mysteries" . . . the little social nuances he never quite seemed to pick up on. *It should not matter to a warrior,* he thought. But somehow it always did.

What do you do when you are inside a human female's cabin and she isn't dressed yet? Should he try to make light conversation? Should he wait in silence? *It's business,* he told himself. *I'm supposed to be here to discuss a mission. The captain sent me. If I stick to business, nothing will go wrong.*

"Make yourself at home," Tasha called. "I'll be right out."

At home. He gave a mental snort. His every nerve was on edge. *If only I knew her better. I . . . could use a friend here.*

Perhaps it was his prickly Klingon nature, but it took him a long time to warm up to strangers. He could tell the rest of the ship's officers were trying their best to get to know each other, to form a real team, and eventually he knew they would all come together. But for now he still felt like an outsider among them, even when they went out of their way to include him in their social banter.

Water splashed. *Is she bathing?* He narrowed his eyes and almost left. *What is she doing in there?*

"If this is a bad time," he began, "I can come back later—"

"No, wait. I'll be right out. Really."

He glanced around her cabin to take his mind off the awkward position he was in. Tasha Yar had brought very few personal effects with her: a scattering of small holographic pictures—planets he didn't recognize, some with Tasha posing next to people he didn't know. In the far corner sat a small Vulcan kinetic sculpture, its thin wire strands dipping faintly in the breeze from the air vents. There was nothing here, nothing special and unique, that proclaimed, *"I am Tasha Yar."*

Perhaps she feels as alone as I do, he thought suddenly. *Perhaps—*

"Sorry about that," Tasha said, emerging from her bedroom and interrupting his thoughts. She wore a slate-gray robe and had a gray towel wrapped around her head. "I was getting ready for my away mission . . . I'm having trouble with my hair. What brings you here?"

"I—" Worf began. He stared as she pulled the towel off her head. Long, straight blond hair spilled out. Hair that didn't belong on her head. "What happened to you—" he burst out.

Instantly he regretted it. It was not an appropriate comment.

"Like it?" She made a face. "It's silly and impractical, if you ask me. I prefer it short."

"But—how—?"

"I borrowed a follicle stimulator from Dr. Crusher." She swept her hair back and out of her eyes with one hand. "Archarian women wear their hair long, unfortunately. Since we're supposed to be going in disguised as natives, I needed to grow it longer to fit in. What do you really think?" She turned a quick pirouette and gave an impish grin. "Stylish?"

"It is . . . *long.*"

She cocked her head quizzically. "I guess that's a compliment."

He swallowed and felt too hot suddenly.

"Wait until you see Commander Riker," she went on with an even broader grin. "Archarian men wear beards . . . long, bushy beards. That's something I'm really looking forward to seeing! He's normally so stiff and formal all the time."

"Unh. Yes. But there is nothing wrong with formality."

"Almost as bad as you."

"Uh—"

"That's supposed to be a joke." She grew more businesslike. "This isn't a social call, is it? What's wrong?"

"Lieutenant . . . we have a situation on the planet's smaller moon." Taking refuge in duty, he began to fill her in on the details. "The captain wants me to lead an away team on a recon mission," he concluded. "He thought it best for me to coordinate with you."

"I see." She nodded somberly. "Worf, you and I both know you're more than capable of dealing with this situation on your own. I'm going to leave it up to you. This is a good chance to impress the captain—don't blow it."

"I have no intention of—*blowing* it." He bristled at the very idea.

"Sorry, sorry, poor choice of words." She hesitated. "Let me suggest a team for you. Take Schultz, Detek, and Wrenn. They've been pulling a lot of extra duty shifts together since Farpoint, and they seem to work well as a team."

"I have already assigned them to this mission—as well as Ensign Clarke."

She raised her eyebrows. "Angling for my job, Worf? I couldn't have picked a better team."

Again he felt the heat rush to his face. "I—uh—"

"Relax, they're good choices. Go with my blessing. Bust some skulls. I know that's what you really want to do."

He gave a curt nod. *My people. Yes, I would like to meet more of my people . . . and bust some skulls!* He felt his blood surge at the thought of combat.

"Thank you—Tasha."

"Don't mention it." She grinned again. "We're all in this together, right?"

Dr. Crusher had her people carefully stationed at all corners of sickbay when Captain Picard strode in with all the subtlety of a hurricane. He did not look pleased at being summoned to sickbay.

"What is so important, Doctor," he said curtly. "We have a possible combat situation developing. My place is on the bridge right now."

"Just this." She took his arm and led him to the virus display. She hadn't changed the image since revealing the hidden message. "Look."

"Smile . . . you are dead?" He frowned. "What is this, Beverly? A joke?"

"That's exactly what I think it is." She nodded at the display. "A private joke. That message is written on the bottom of every single virus. It's been coded into the NXA protein strands."

He frowned. "Then it *is* artificial—"

"Created from Rhulian flu, and almost certainly by a human."

"I don't want to believe it. I—" He licked his lips. "I think—"

It was the first time she had seen him this way in years. *Since Jack died,* she thought. *Since that awful, awful day when my husband died.*

"We don't know who did it. He didn't sign his name. But I have a suspicion."

"Tell me."

"Dr. Tang, the head of Archo City Hospital. His specialty is virology, and to all indications he's very, very good . . . cutting-edge good."

"Do you have evidence of this?"

"No. It's just a feeling I have from talking with him—a feeling that he's doing his best to stonewall my research. I think he has some serious mental instabilities, and judging from his comments, he would fit right in with the Purity League. He wants the planet quarantined and left on its own permanently."

"These are very serious charges."

"I know. And I don't have any proof yet."

He hesitated, staring at the virus, at the letters on its underside. "Does the technology necessary to create this virus exist anywhere else on Archaria III *besides* Dr. Tang's hospital?"

"I doubt it. You would need a state-of-the-art

research lab . . . and advanced knowledge of human and nonhuman virology."

Slowly Picard nodded. "You may be right. It would certainly help explain why Tang hasn't made any progress toward a cure."

Dr. Crusher nodded. *He wants them dead. Why create a cure for your own plague?*

"I'll alert Commander Riker to your suspicions—he may be able to turn up more information on Tang during his away mission." He cleared his throat. "Who else knows about this message?"

"So far, just the people here. I ordered them to keep it to themselves."

"Good. We don't want a panic on the planet. Are you any closer to a cure?"

"We're just starting to unravel the NXA protein threads holding the virus together. There's no telling what nasty little tricks our genetic programmer tucked into it."

Captain Picard gave a pensive nod. "Thank you, Doctor. You did the right thing. Keep me up to date on your progress." He paused. "You *can* cure it, can't you?"

"I think so, eventually. It's just a matter of time. Unfortunately, that's the one thing we're short of."

"Keep at it. Thousands are counting on you." Turning, he headed for the door.

As if we don't have enough pressure already.

After the doors whisked shut, Dr. Crusher took a deep breath. "All right," she called to her people. "Gather around. We have a lot of work to do."

She started handing out assignments: NXA sequencing, tests with antiviral compounds, analyses of the protein strands within the virus.

We will *get to the bottom of this mess,* she told herself. *And it's going to be sooner rather than later—Dr. Tang and his stonewalling be damned!*

Chapter Seven

FIFTEEN MINUTES AFTER his conversation with Tasha Yar, Worf met the four members of his away team in Transporter Room 3. Like them, he had changed into a full containment suit. The bulky white garment felt suffocating, but it covered him completely from head to heel. No virus would get through it. *I might as well be in a full spacesuit,* he thought.

He felt an itch starting in the middle of his back and gave a growl of displeasure. *Klingons are not meant for containment suits.* And as he continued to breathe, his faceplate fogged over. What had his instructor at the Academy told him to do when that happened? *Practice your breathing—keep it slow and steady.* Hyperventilating caused it.

He nudged the comm bar with his chin. A

channel opened up to the other members of his away team.

"Since we will be beaming into potentially hostile territory," he said, letting a grim note creep into his voice, "you must be on your guard at *all* times. Watch your backs, no matter what you see or hear. And remember . . ." He paused for emphasis. "This *is* a good day to die!"

That did it. The ensign swallowed noticeably.

Worf gave a mental snort. *Humans.* It really *was* a good day to die. If you went into combat fearing nothing, you walked the path to glory.

He had already selected their beam-in coordinates: an unoccupied dome on the far edge of the research station. La Forge's last sensor scans had placed all the humans and Klingons a safe distance away, in the buildings nearer to the station's landing pad, so their arrival should go unnoticed. His plan called for securing the dome, then using it as a base of operations as they made their way through the complex slowly and methodically, searching for victims. Their first priority would be reaching the man La Forge had spotted.

"Take your positions for transport!" he barked.

His team scrambled onto the transporter pad. They arranged themselves in a semicircle, leaving the middle pad open for him. He took it, turned, and faced the ensign on duty at the transporter controls.

"Energize!" he said, loud enough to be heard even through his helmet.

As lights began to sparkle around him, the *Enter-*

prise disappeared . . . and was replaced by a dimly lit room perhaps twenty meters high and forty meters across. The white ceiling arched overhead in a huge dome.

Artificial gravity was on; it felt just under Earth normal to Worf. He dropped to a crouch, phaser rifle up and ready. Scans might show a room empty . . . but shields had been known to hide ambushes, and he never took unnecessary chances.

There was no ambush this time. Around him lay jumbles of boxes, huge wooden packing crates, and discarded machinery. The crates rose in teetering stacks, some of them nearly reached the ceiling.

No danger. Or nothing that leaped out with fangs bared and claws ready, he thought. Diseases were far more insidious than that.

"Guard duty." He motioned Schultz to the rear hatch and Clarke to the front. "Secure the dome," he said. "Shout if anyone tries to get in. Do not shoot unless fired upon or I give the word."

"Yes, sir!" They hurried to take up their positions. Only then did Worf relax enough take his finger off his own phaser's firing button.

Wrenn had his tricorder out. Turning slowly, the ensign scanned the dome.

"No other life forms within thirty meters," he reported over the open channel. "The nearest life signs are from two humans located exactly thirty-two meters due north—that way." He pointed toward the front of the dome, just to the right of Clarke's position.

"Are they moving?" Worf asked.

"No, sir. From their life signs, I think they're either asleep or unconscious."

Or dying from the plague, Worf thought. He sucked in a deep breath. *Do not hyperventilate.*

"Keep monitoring them," he said. "Let me know if their status changes. And keep watch for anyone else moving in our direction."

Perhaps this would be easier than he had first thought. If everyone was sick, they would not offer resistance to the rescue mission. The Klingons here would not be affected by the plague, he reminded himself. Nor would any full-blooded humans.

First, he had to address the problem at hand: securing this dome. Frowning a little, he regarded the stacks of boxes and crates all around him. Clearly the people in charge of this base had used this chamber as their storage area . . . or their dump. The crates bore labels like "Thermoentogram Modulator B-6" and "Dioxymosis Converter (F)," whatever those were. To the left, a few of the boxes made more sense: "Vegetable Concentrate 64" and "2400 Citric Protein Bars" sounded almost sensible in comparison, if not exactly appetizing. Sometimes he thought humans would eat anything, if it came in an attractive package.

First things first, though. The jumble of crates might conceal anything from a cloaked Romulan death squad to a the lost treasures of *Fret'vok.* If they planned on using this dome as a base of operations, they were going to have to search it fully—you couldn't cover your back if you didn't know what was behind you.

"Look behind the boxes on that side of the room," he told Detek and Wrenn. "If you see anything unusual, let me know immediately. Do not investigate yourselves."

"Yes, sir!"

Turning with a sigh, Worf squeezed between a pair of tall "Emulsion Generator" crates. His containment suit snagged for a second on a nail, but since the material couldn't be punctured by anything as soft as mere steel, he pulled sharply and felt himself snap free.

Whoever had packed all this junk into the dome had left less-than-adequate access corridors between the piles of crates. He edged down the nearest one and felt himself treading on things that crunched underfoot.

His phaser rifle had a small but powerful light mounted on top; he flicked it on, then swept the beam up and down the floor. Loose cables, discarded circuit relays, food wrappers, and other trash littered the floor here. From the thick layer of dust on everything, he knew no one had been back here in many years.

He had just turned to go back when Wrenn's excited voice squealed his name: *"Lieutenant Worf!"*

"What is it?" he demanded. Had the Klingons from the freighter detected them and launched at attack?

"Sir!" he heard Wrenn call. *"We found something! Blood—and according to my tricorder, it's human!"*

"Hold your position. I will be right there."

Somehow he managed to squeeze back out into the center of the dome without tumbling any of the piles of crates. He spotted Wrenn about halfway to the front door and sprinted over to join him.

The ensign pointed to dark stains on the floor. "According to my tricorder, that's human blood," he said. "It's dry, but fresh—about twelve hours old!"

Worf bent to examine the blood spatters. A trail of blood wound off between crates on that side of the dome. He hesitated, trying to decide how best to handle it.

"Is it fully human?" he finally asked. "Or is it a human-Peladian mix?" *One of the symptoms of the disease is uncontrollable bleeding,* he reminded himself.

Wrenn had to check. "Uh . . . fully human, sir. Not a trace of Peladian genetic material."

So we have the trail of a wounded human. Hefting his phaser rifle, Worf eased between crates of "Endochronic Thiotimoline Pumps" and "Phase Resonance Detectors." His heart began to pound with growing excitement. Shining his light at the floor, he studied the footprints and the blood. The drips became noticeably larger, and bloody handprints smeared the crates to either side where someone had rested or leaned to steady himself.

When the passageway opened up a little, he

spotted at least three—and possibly as many as five—different sets of footprints that had disturbed the decades' worth of accumulated dust . . . whoever had come through here made no effort to conceal the trail. *They could not all be dead or dying,* Worf thought with growing unease. His eyes narrowed. *What happened here?*

He continued to follow the trail, winding between the crates and boxes. At last he reached the far wall.

The trail ended with a pool of sticky, half-congealed blood. And lying in that blood he found the bodies of six adult human males. Acharian settlers, he decided, noting their chest-length beards. He remembered what Tasha Yar had told him about the men on Archaria III all wearing long, bushy beards.

These six had been stabbed and cut repeatedly. The blood came from their wounds. But they had not died here—someone had carefully arranged the bodies. Eyes closed, hands neatly folded across their chests, they looked almost peaceful now. The trail he had followed must have been left by a burial party, he decided.

Better to die in honorable combat than to succumb to a disease, he thought with a nod. Unless they had been murdered. . . .

He moved closer and began to study the bodies with the dispassionate attention of a born predator. Death had been sudden, but not unexpected, he decided. He pulled their shredded tunics open to study their wounds. Two had numerous stab wounds.

Those cuts—

He leaned forward, studying the long, clean sweep of the death blows. A strong arm had delivered those cuts. The wounds looked exactly like the marks left by a mek'leth. *Or in this case, several mek'leths.*

Only Klingons used that particular type of short sword, he knew, with its razor-sharp edge and deadly point—perfect for slashing and thrusting. He liked to use one himself. Unlike disruptors, it made combat a personal experience . . . but it also made for messy corpses. *Exactly like these.*

Lights wavered behind him as the ensigns followed. Over the open comm channel he heard gasps of shock from Wrenn and Detek.

"Control yourself," he snarled. "You must have seen death before."

"Not like this," Wrenn gasped.

"All that blood," Detek said.

"What's going on?" Clarke demanded from his post by the front hatch. *"Do you need assistance? Lieutenant? Anybody?"*

"Quiet on the channel." Worf rose and pivoted on the balls of his feet, furious with the breaches in protocol. *This is going in their personal files,* he vowed. Simpering over a little blood!

He found Wrenn, pale-faced, two meters away, just standing there and staring open-mouthed at the bodies.

"Back to the center of the dome!" he said.

The ensign began to stammer in shock or fear.

"Go on!" Worf grimaced with distaste. *No stomach for a little blood!* He switched off his rifle's light, hiding the gruesome details. Perhaps that would help. *They are only humans,* he reminded himself. *They cannot help their weaknesses.* Still, he had expected more from them. After all, he was leading this mission.

"Go back to the center of the dome," he ordered a little more gently. "Wait there and keep it clear in case we have to return."

Worf clicked his comm bar back to the first setting so that he could talk to the "survivors" of his mission.

"Detek," he said, voice a low growl.

"Sir!" The ensign's voice quavered noticeably.

"Get the tricorder and medical supplies. You are now our rear guard."

Turning, he headed for the front hatch without a backward glance. *The other three will pull together and pick up the slack,* he thought. He hoped.

Chapter Eight

DR. CRUSHER PASSED OUT ASSIGNMENTS, and as her people scrambled to work on unraveling the secrets of the virus, she took a minute to page Dr. Tang at Archo City Hospital. *This should prove interesting,* she thought. *Let's see how he reacts to news of that hidden message.* Maybe it would force his hand . . . or surprise him into an admission of guilt.

Tang finally answered the page. "What is it?" he growled. *Still practicing Dracula's bedside manner, I see,* Dr. Crusher thought. *Only this time I know your real motive.*

She said: "Dr. Tang, I have isolated the virus and done a complete TXA breakdown. In the process, I found something quite disturbing—not only is the virus man-made, but its designer left a message."

"What!" He stared at her, to all appearances shocked. "What's the message?"

"Smile, you are dead." She gave him the NXA strand number. "Sequence it yourself. When you pull back the view, watch the bottom of the tendril. The modified texture spells it out clearly."

He sucked in a deep breath. "Doctor—I can't believe it! The Purity League claimed responsibility for the plague, but I never thought . . . I never dreamed . . . they actually had the resources to do it!"

If he was acting, he deserved a commendation for it. She hadn't seen a better job since the time she saw Sir Edmund Deere in *Hamlet* on Earth.

I should have asked Deanna to join me for this conference, she realized with a pang of disappointment. *Deanna would have sensed if he told us the truth.* She felt foolish for wasting the call. *I'll do it next time,* she vowed. *Until I know differently, you are still my prime suspect, Doctor!*

"Our captain wants this information kept strictly confidential," she said.

"Of course—I do understand."

He appeared humbled by the revelation, she thought. But then, if as he claimed he really *had* been working on the virus for weeks, he hadn't found that hidden message . . . and she turned it up within the hour. *Don't get too cocky,* she told herself. *It was luck. But luck is what you sometimes need.*

Tang went on, "I must tell the governor, though . . . but of course he won't dare release the information to anyone else. The repercussions would be disastrous. As your captain must already realize."

She nodded. Riots. Open warfare. And the pure-blooded Peladians would almost certainly get involved; how could they not? The next custom-made virus might well target *them.*

She said, "Getting back to our real problem—curing the plague—I'm ready to bring an infected test subject aboard."

"You have a vaccine already?" He leaned forward eagerly. "How does it work—can I get a sample—"

"No, we don't have a vaccine yet," she said quickly. She was finding it increasingly difficult to believe he was guilty. His every response seemed genuine and correct. "We have some other tests to run first. The virus appears to be a simple variant of Rhulian flu. We have some antiviral treatments specifically designed for that disease which might prove effective."

He sighed and shook his head. "The virus does appear simple at first glance, Doctor." *Back to stonewalling and doomsaying,* she thought. *How true to form.* "However, it cannot be cured by any traditional means—we tried all the Rhulian flu vaccines as well as every other antiviral agent known to the Federation. The virus resisted every treatment—it's all in the research notes I sent you. Every time we thought we had it licked, it flared up again."

"Yes, I read your report. But I have a clean

environment here, and I have a crew working on modifying the biofilters in the transporters." *At least, I will as soon as this call is done.* "An aggressive program using several different treatments should prove successful."

"I hope so—for your sake." Tang shook his head. "We had no luck there, either, Doctor. But perhaps the *Enterprise*'s biofilters are more advanced than our own."

"Undoubtedly." Crusher hoped O'Brien knew what he was doing. "We have some . . . *creative* engineers aboard. If they can see the virus, they can eliminate it. It's that simple."

Tang shrugged helplessly. "I hope so, Doctor," he said. "I will have that test patient standing by. Please—for your own sake, maintain a quarantine field at all times. This virus really does jump the strongest forcefields."

"Of course," she said. "I intend to use every security measure at my disposal."

"Then I will await news of your ultimate success." He hesitated. "And Doctor . . ."

"Yes?" she said.

"I know how I must seem to you. You must think I'm a crackpot a . . . a medical *alarmist*, since I keep trying to poke holes in every theory and plan you come up with. Believe me when I say I *do* want a cure—I want it more desperately than you can possibly imagine! But I don't want to risk the lives of anyone healthy to get it, and that includes your crew."

"Thank you for your concern," she said. *I bet it gets even more heartfelt every time he tells that story.* "I do appreciate your advice. I have no intention of placing this crew at risk. Now, please get that patient ready. I'll want to beam him up within the hour."

"You will have him," he said, almost humbly.

"Crusher out."

Now to make sure we live up to our reputation, she thought. She tapped her combadge.

"Crusher to Transporter Chief O'Brien."

"O'Brien here, ma'am," came his answer.

"About those biofilters you mentioned this morning. How long will it take you to chain them together?"

She heard a distinct gulp on the other end of the comm channel. *Good,* she thought with satisfaction.

"No problem, ma'am!" O'Brien said.

"That's the kind of answer I like, O'Brien. Crusher out!"

On the bridge, Captain Picard faced the forward viewscreen and watched the *Constitution* enter the solar system with a measure of relief. Captain van Osterlich's ship had arrived not an hour too soon, he thought. With a second Galaxy-class starship to help keep order, he felt a little more relaxed. *We can go chasing after rogue ships now, if we have to,* he thought. There was no longer any need to worry about leaving the planet unguarded.

"Hail the *Constitution*," he said.

"Captain van Osterlich is standing by," La Forge said.

"On screen."

The view of Archaria III disappeared, replaced by the smiling face of Jules van Osterlich, its captain. Van Osterlich had broad cheekbones and thin hair so pale it looked almost white.

Picard grinned back. They had known each other the better part of twenty years. Though their careers kept them half a galaxy apart most of the time, they never passed up an opportunity to get together and talk about the good old days.

"Jean-Luc!" van Osterlich said. "The new ship suits you. I always knew you'd end up with one of the big ones. But the *Enterprise!* Quite a plum."

"Thank you, Jules. The *Constitution*'s looking pretty good, too. A fine ship."

"That she is."

"How long has it been . . . three years? Four? How are you?"

"I can't complain. So, I hear we have quite a situation developing below. Why don't you fill me in. My transporter crews are ready to beam medical supplies down, but we have a few minutes before we enter orbit."

"Dinner tonight? Bring your senior staff."

"Delighted."

"Good." Picard frowned. "We'll talk more then," he said. "In the meantime, you should know that things below are not quite what they appear. Governor Sekk has, ah, held out on us. And we suspect some of the hospital staff may be hindering the development of a cure for the plague in support of the Purity League. My chief medical officer is spearheading the research aboard the *Enterprise.*"

"And what is happening with the plague?"

"Latest reports indicate forty thousand victims. Three quarters of them are already dead. It isn't a pretty situation."

Van Osterlich whistled. "It's a disaster!" He glanced over his shoulder. "Governor Sekk is hailing me," he said. "We'll talk more tonight."

Picard nodded. "I'll break out the Saurian brandy."

Chapter Nine

"SECURE THE AREA!" Worf barked.

After kicking open the hatch to the next dome—it housed a research station complete with humming, beeping, chirping weather-monitoring equipment—he led the charge inside. Detek's tricorder showed two humans lying in the center of a cluster of three rooms. Asleep? Unconscious? Lying in ambush? He intended to find out.

He pointed: Schultz left, Clarke right. He went straight up the middle, treading as softly as a Klingon could.

He reached the door to the next room, pressed up beside it, and reached out to the handpad, which was unlocked. He pressed lightly, and it zipped to one side.

Taking a glance in, he spotted two figures lying in

semi darkness . . . both women. He switched on the lights, but neither one moved.

Plague. White blisters covered their faces. *That's one of the first signs.*

"Sir, is it—?" Clarke asked over the comm.

"Yes." His voice came as a growl. "They have the plague. That means the whole base is contaminated."

For the first time since beaming down, he was thankful they were inside containment suits. Like Wrenn, they would have to be beamed out of them when they were evacuated.

He clicked the comm bar.

"Worf to Dr. Crusher. . . ."

"Crusher here," she replied an instant later. *"What is your situation?"*

"The plague is loose in here. We have found two victims so far. Both women."

"What are their symptoms?"

"White blisters on their faces. Low life signs. They are both unconscious."

He heard a slight hesitation in her voice. *"Mark their coordinates. We are almost ready to try beaming a patient through the ship's biofilters. We'll try your women if it works on our first subject."*

"Good." He felt a brief surge of pride. By coming here, they had already made a difference— these two women would have a chance for survival now.

"Are there any other plague victims?"

"Not yet," he said. "We will continue to investigate the base."

"Keep me up to date. Crusher out."

Worf turned to Ensign Detek. "Send the coordinates for these two to sickbay," he said. "And scan for more survivors."

"Yes, sir."

Detek raised his tricorder and turned slowly, scanning. "Five more humans are in the dome immediately to our left," he said. "The Klingons are still forty meters to the right."

Worf hesitated. Which group to contact first? *The humans,* he thought. *They are the most threatened by the plague.*

"We will investigate the humans first," he announced. "Let us go!"

He led the way to the back of the dome, opened the hatch into the ten-meter-long connective walkway, and advanced cautiously to the next hatch.

He pressed the handpad, but although it beeped, it stubbornly refused to open . . . locked from the inside, he decided.

"What is the status of the humans inside?" he asked.

"They are . . . alive and moving, sir. I believe they have detected us. They are taking up positions around the door."

Around the door? *Ambush!*

"Get down!" he ordered. "Rifles up!"

He clicked the comm bar and called the *Enterprise.* "I need an emergency site-to-site transport!"

he yelled. "Put us inside the dome we're facing! On the farthest side!"

"Ready, sir," he heard an unfamiliar voice say.

The hatch started to open.

"Energize!"

As the transporter beam picked them up, he saw the flash of energy weapons being fired—

—and suddenly he and his men were materializing inside the dome, facing a curving white wall. He whirled. They hadn't gone far—twenty meters at the most—but they were in a different room now.

He charged the half-shut door. Bursting through, he launched himself into the main chamber.

Five people stood with their backs to him, and two of them had disruptors pointed out toward the open hatch. He recognized the corridor where he and his men had been standing seconds before.

The men with the disruptors started to turn. *Too late!* Worf thought with the glee of a predator closing in for the kill. He felt the roar of his blood. He voiced a wordless battle cry, *"A-a-a-a-r-h—"*

Before they could shoot him, he fired from his hip. *Heavy stun*—first the two men with the weapons, the one on the left, then the one on the right.

Even as they began to crumple, he closed the distance between in a heartbeat, still yelling, *"—a-a-a-a-h—"*

The other three—two men, a woman—were not armed. His Starfleet training took over and Worf dragged himself back from the berserker's abyss. It would have been easy to let himself go in the fury and passion of the moment, to kill and kill again while his blood sang the music of violence in his ears.

Panting, he halted before them. "Arms up!" he bellowed. He knew his voice carried through his faceplate when he shouted—it would be a little muffled, but clearly audible.

The three standing humans gaped at him, too shocked to move. They did not seem to be armed.

"Arms up, I said! I *will* shoot!"

This time they raised their arms.

Bending at the knees, he scooped up the disruptors dropped by the two men. *Set to kill,* he noticed. His ensigns took guard positions.

"Identify yourselves!" he snapped.

"My name is Newkirk," one of the men snarled. He was an older human with short gray hair. *No beard. Not from Archaria III.* "I am first officer of the *Middlemarch.* You just killed the captain, you Klingon bastard!"

Worf glared. "I am Lieutenant Worf of the Federation starship *Enterprise,*" he snapped back. "Your captain is stunned."

"You're a Klingon!" the other man said suspiciously. "What kind of trick is this?"

"I am a Starfleet officer. Identify yourself!"

"Macus Onetree," he said flatly, "second officer of the *Middlemarch.* About time you got here, Starfleet. We've needed rescue for three days. Those Klingons have attacked us twice."

"Explain."

Onetree hesitated. "Plague broke out on the planet, so we bugged it up to orbit. Captain Gorman"—he indicated one of the men Worf had shot—"thought we should ride out the problems here. He remembered this deserted base, so . . ." He snorted. "Between Klingons sniping at us, half our crew dropping dead from the plague, and our warp drive breaking down—what else can possibly go wrong?"

Worf gave a nod and lowered his phaser rifle. "How many dead from plague?" he asked.

"All but us five now. The others are in the next dome."

He nudged the comm bar with his chin. *That is easy enough to check,* he thought.

"Worf to La Forge."

"La Forge here," came the answer.

"How many life signs are now on this base?"

"Hold on . . . twenty-two."

Ten Klingons, five humans here, two in the other dome—that's only seventeen. The other five must be the governor's family. He gave a nod. That accounted for everyone.

"Have you met anyone else here besides the Klingons?" he asked.

"There are more humans holed up in one of the domes . . . they sealed the doors and they won't come out. They threatened to shoot anyone who came near, so we haven't bothered them. Since the Klingons smashed the base's comm equipment, we haven't been able to reach them."

They are better off locked in their dome, Worf

thought. *These people may be immune because they are full humans, but they are carrying the virus.*

"You will stay here," he told them. "When your captain wakes up, inform him that he is under house arrest pending an investigation. Attacking Federation officers is still a crime."

"You're not going to leave us here!" Onetree cried.

Now he wants to be rescued. Worf snorted.

"You are welcome to come with me," he said. "I am going to see the Klingons next."

Chapter Ten

ONLY THE TRANSPORTER CHIEF'S LEGS remained visible as he crawled into the transporter's console. *Does he know what he's doing?* Dr. Crusher wondered, and not for the first time. This seemed a highly irregular way to adjust the biofilters. As she watched, his knees bent. His feet pointed, twitched, pointed again. And he crawled another twenty centimeters into the console.

"Are you sure you should be doing that?" Dr. Crusher asked. She had always been told to bring power off-line before adjusting relays. *It's got to be dangerous.*

"I've done it a thousand times before, ma'am," O'Brien said, sounding put-upon. "There are so many safety features and redundancies built in, it's physically impossible for me to get hurt—*Ow!*"

"Are you all right?"

"YES!" he bellowed. Then she heard him swear under his breath as something thumped loudly inside the console. *"Get in there!"*

Dr. Crusher wavered between calling for help and crawling in after him.

She jumped when an electric sizzle sounded and a curl of acrid black smoke rose from the control pads. She took a step back in alarm. *He doesn't know what he's doing!* she thought. *He's crazy!*

Another thump came, even louder than the first. The transporter chief gave another yelp and jerked back, feet spasming, and then he crawled out, alternately waving his fingers in the air and sucking on them.

"Are you all right?" she asked, one hand reaching instinctively for her medical tricorder. "Maybe I should take a look at that—"

"No need, Doc." He grinned up at her. "My own bloody stupidity. I touched the wrong relay."

Muttering to himself, he stuck his head under the console again. The sizzle came again, then disappeared as he undid whatever he had done before. A second plume of black smoke rose. She caught a whiff of something burning. *I really ought to call for backup—*

"Just an overloaded circuit," he said, as if that explained everything. "No need to worry."

"Oh." Dr. Crusher leaned over, trying to see what he was doing under there. *How can he see in there? It's pitch black. If he electrocuted himself—*

"Almost got it." One hand suddenly stuck out toward her. "Pass me that magnetic lock, will you, ma'am?"

"Coming." It sat on top of the control panel with half a dozen other tools. She grabbed it and smacked it into his palm like a nurse handing a doctor a medical instrument. *Ten years since I've done that!* She raised her tricorder and tried to scan those burned fingers, but he pulled his hand back under the console again before she caught more than a glimpse. *Probably a minor flash burn. He may have brushed a live EM conduit,* she thought, trying to dredge up old equipment-maintenance lessons from memory. *It's painful, but not serious. I'll send him some ointment later.*

Something creaked alarmingly under the console, like bones about to break. It sounded worse than anything else O'Brien had yet done.

"Unh . . . almost . . . there!"

The lights on the control panel flickered, then went out.

"Bloody hell!"

"Maybe I should call someone from engineering to assist you—" she began.

He stuck his head out and positively glared at her. *"Don't.* Ma'am. Beggin' your pardon, but I'd never hear the end of it! I've got my *pride,* you know."

"Lives are at stake here—"

"I know, and the sooner I shut up and get back to work, the sooner you'll get 'em saved." He disappeared into the console again.

Territorial, these engineering types. She sighed. At this point, it was probably best to let him do his work.

"Why don't they build these things to standard specs?" she heard O'Brien mutter to himself. "You'd think a Galaxy-class starship would use the same C-22a transporter-buffer configuration as the rest of the fleet, wouldn't you? But *no,* that's not good enough. Some bright kid decides it's better to start over from scratch and reinvent the wheel, and we're the ones who suffer for it. . . ."

Something creaked again. The lights flickered, came on, died, flickered, and died again. And then they didn't come on at all.

Dr. Crusher signed. *Twelve minutes. Three more, then I call Engineering.*

"How's that?" he asked from inside. "Everything look okay?"

"It's completely dead."

"Eh? *Still?*" he called. Something made a banging sound, like steel on steel. Dr. Crusher winced. *He's insane. I'm trusting my patient—and the safety of the crew—to a madman.*

"Just a minute more!" he called.

"Are you *sure* this is going to work?"

"Of course." He grunted again. He pounded on something. He cursed. But finally the console lights came back on and a familiar hum of power filled the room.

"That does it." The transporter chief pulled his red-haired head out and gave her a winning smile.

"Knew I'd get it in the end. I've manually cross-chained two transporter buffers, so you'll get a double-strength biofilter. No virus is going to make it through there unless *we* want it to. Just give the word, Doc, and I'll start the transport."

"Okay." Something made her hesitate, though. She still had her doubts about jerry-rigged transporters. It might do in a true emergency, but when the safety of the crew lay at stake, when a potentially lethal virus might make it on board, she wanted something extra. Strange creaking noises and flickering power supplies did *not* engender confidence, she thought.

That's why we're beaming into a level-1 containment field, she thought. Even if he screwed up the biofilters, nothing would get loose on the ship.

"Let's give it a try."

She tapped her badge. "Crusher to Dr. Tang."

"Tang here," he replied almost instantly. *He must have been waiting for my call.*

"Do you have that patient ready?"

"Yes. Lock onto the other person at these coordinates—"

Crusher glanced at O'Brien, who nodded.

"Bring him aboard," she said.

"He's in the pattern buffer," Transporter Chief O'Brien said. "Now . . . applying the first set of biofilter algorhithms . . . now the second set . . . done!"

It's too easy, she thought. *If this worked, Dr. Tang would have cured all his patients by now.* Unless he only managed to reinfect them. Unless he sabotaged his own work to help the Purity League. *No virus can make it through the biofilters,* she thought. *It has to work. It's medically impossible for it* not *to work.*

"Leave him in the pattern buffer until I have the containment field set up," she said, starting for sickbay. "I'll let you know when we're ready."

"Got it, ma'am!"

Five minutes later, the hum of a transporter beam filled the sickbay. Dr. Crusher and her staff gathered around biobed 1 and the forcefield now shimmering there.

A woman materialized on the bed. She had long, flowing black hair, an elongated Peladian skull, and white blisters covering her face, neck, and hands.

Dr. Crusher raised her tricorder and began a quick scan. The virus was gone. *So much for Dr. Tang,* she thought. As far as she was concerned, this proved he had been lying all along. *Now, all we have to do is find an antiviral agent that works,* she thought, *and begin mass-producing it.*

"We have a winner," she announced. "The virus is gone."

Her staff let loose a cheer.

Smiling, she lowered her tricorder. "All we need is a vaccine and we'll be set. How is it coming?"

"I think we'll have something in a few hours. We're running cultures now. All indications are positive—we'll have that cure by the end of the day. It's only Rhulian flu, after all."

Dr. Crusher nodded. "Prepare two more bio-beds," she said to her nurses. "We have patients on the moon to bring across."

It looked like the start of a very busy afternoon.

She continued to monitor her plague patient, listening to the steady beat of her heart on the biobed's monitor. Within twenty minutes, the woman's fever was gone. Within an hour, the fever blisters on her face had begun to shrink noticeably. Blood tests, sensor scans, and every medical instrument in sickbay revealed her to be a healthy young adult female in every way.

Too bad we can't beam every patient on the planet through our biofilters, she thought. *But even with all our transporters working around the clock—even if you count the* Constitution—*we would barely get one or two percent of the victims processed. And we would have to start beaming them back down to the planet because we'd run out of room here . . . and they would be reinfected immediately.*

No, they needed a real cure. That was the only solution.

Even so, Dr. Crusher found it hard to restrain her jubilation. It wasn't every day she had such immediate and gratifying results from a treatment. So much for Dr. Tang and all his dire warnings.

"Get back to work on the vaccine," she said.

Deanna Troi strolled in shortly thereafter. "I

heard you have a new patient, Beverly," she said. "I can tell by the glow on your face that the news is good. Is she awake yet?"

"Not yet . . . but soon." Smiling, Dr. Crusher led the way to biobed 1. The white fever blisters had almost all vanished on the woman's face. "As you can see, she's still unconscious. I didn't want to administer a stimulant yet . . . rest is the best thing for her right now."

Deanna leaned close to the forcefield. "She's dreaming. I sense some very turbulent emotions . . . do you have a case history on her? I'd like to read it before we talk."

"No—and I'm sure the Archo City Hospital doesn't have one, either. They've been overwhelmed by the thousands of plague victims. They didn't even bother sending paperwork up with her—we don't even know her name."

Deanna sighed, but nodded. "All right. I want to be here when she wakes up, though. She's going to need counseling to deal with her trauma. Promise you'll call me?"

"Of course." That was the least they could do for their patient. Mental as well as physical health—a doctor had to worry about both.

Deanna gazed silently at the woman. "Is that forcefield still necessary?" she asked.

"For now. It's a standard safety procedure." *And I promised Dr. Tang—he insisted the virus leaped through biofilters. But when there isn't a virus present, it can't leap through anything, can it? She* gave a mental snort. *All those lies . . . I wonder how he sleeps at night. First things first. Once the plague is under control, I'll make sure charges are pressed against him . . . if not on Archaria III, then on a Federation world in a Federation court.*

The Federation took charges of genocide very seriously.

PART 2:
The Plague Escapes

Interlude

SUNSET OVER ARCHO CITY dazzled the eyes with brilliant fingers of red and pink and gold. Solomon studied the spectacular colors as he waited impatiently for his ground transportation to arrive. *No pollution. No air traffic. Not a person in sight . . . I might be the last person in this whole world,* he thought.

Faint in the distance, a truck rumbled somewhere behind him, breaking the spell. He sighed and glanced around impatiently. Where was his car? It should have been here by now.

I'm a grain buyer. Even in the midst of panic and chaos, they bend over backwards to serve me. He found a certain irony in the fact that he had pretty much destroyed the social fabric of their world. *Not that it was particularly worth saving.*

"Aren't you afraid of the plague?" the elderly desk clerk had asked him that afternoon when he came down for an early supper. He saw not another soul in the lobby, nor were any patrons eating in the hotel restaurant. *Rats leaving a sinking ship,* he thought with an inward chuckle. *Only with the planet quarantined, they have no place to go.*

"The plague? Not really," Solomon told him matter-of-factly. "I haven't had a sick day in my life, and I'm not going to start now."

"We have begun relocating most of our off-world guests to rural inns. We think they will be safer there, between the plague and the Purity League unrest. If you'd like, we can have your baggage packed while you're out—"

"No, thank you. I prefer to stay here."

"But the plague—"

"A minor inconvenience, that's all." He gave a dismissive gesture. "I'm sure either the Federation or your own excellent hospital system will soon have it sorted out. Besides, I thought only mixers were affected by it. I'm certainly not half Peladian!"

"Obviously, sir. So far, only those damn mixers have caught it, lucky for us humans."

"Oh?" *I know where your sympathies lie, poor old fool.* Feigning interest, Solomon asked, "Have you heard anything else about the plague? Like who's really responsible?"

"Not really . . . just a few rumors." The clerk licked his lips and leaned forward, voice dropping to a conspiratorial whisper. "They say the Federation is terrified that the disease is going to mutate and take us humans next. The Peladians made it, you know, in their secret laboratories."

Solomon stared at him incredulously. "No!" It was all he could do to keep from bursting out laughing. *The Peladians!* Oh, it was too funny. The Purity League certainly moved swiftly to put its own spin on the plague virus. *Everyone wants to take credit for it but me.*

"Yes, sir. It's true. That's exactly what I heard."

"Well, until I catch it myself, I'm not going to believe it. Now, can you check on my transport? It was supposed to be here by now."

And you really don't *want to see me when I'm annoyed,* he added mentally.

"At once, sir." Turning, the clerk hurried to a comm terminal in the back office.

Solomon leaned on the counter, listening with half an ear as the clerk yelled at some poor dispatcher. He hadn't realized how quickly a planet's infrastructure could collapse. *Less than 5 percent of the planet is susceptible to the virus, and everyone's acting like it's the end of the universe.*

A moment later, the clerk returned. "All the drivers called in sick today," he reported. "When I explained how important you were, Joshua Teague himself—Teague's the owner—promised to send his son with a vehicle for you. Best they have, he said. His son, Berke, is a good boy. I've known him for years. He won't let you down."

"Thank you."

"Best of all," the clerk went on, "they're only

going to charge you the economy rental rates—to make up for your inconvenience, sir."

"It doesn't matter. I'm on an expense account." *The General is paying for it, after all,* Solomon thought. "I appreciate the trouble Mr. Teague is going to on my behalf. Please make sure he bills the full amount to my room here."

"Of course, sir!" The clerk looked overjoyed. *He'll probably take half of it for his own services,* Solomon thought with amusement. He had never been one to begrudge lowly employees their share of graft. *After all, that's what keeps the universe afloat.*

"How long will it take?" he asked. "It's getting dark, and I *am* in something of a hurry."

"It will be here momentarily, sir. Would you care for a complimentary drink while you wait? If you like, I can have it brought out to the lobby for you—"

"No, thank you. I think I'll wait outside."

"If you must, sir." The clerk didn't seem to like that idea, but Solomon didn't particularly care. After all, what could possibly happen?

He strolled through the deserted lobby and out to the deserted sidewalk and looked around the deserted square. None of the shops had opened today. But the black marble fountains burbled happily, and small grayish birds—real Earth pigeons, by their look—strutted happily this way and that. He watched, and studied the magnificent sunset as it colored the west with a brilliant palette.

At last a small luxury aircar settled to the ground in front of the hotel. It was a Praxx Cruiser, a couple of years old but once the very top of their line. Ten meters long and three meters high, its body had been elegantly sculpted along aerodynamic lines. Its shiny black paint job gleamed with fresh polish.

Not bad, Solomon decided, ambling over to inspect it. The last aircar they'd sent him had been a twenty-year-old Junco Jett. *Certainly much better than I expected.* If the Cruiser handled half as well as it looked, he would be one happy customer.

A bearded young man opened the side doors and climbed out. He did *not* look happy, though. He kept glancing around the square as though half expecting mobs of screaming Peladians to attack at any moment.

"You must be Buck Teague." Solomon smiled cheerfully and offered his hand. "Thanks for coming."

"It's Berke, sir." Berke shook hands, looking even unhappier. *Probably terrified he's going to catch something from me,* Solomon thought with growing amusement. *Everyone deals with a plague differently.*

Berke turned and pointed into the driver's compartment. "Autopilot, navigator console, manual controls, computer controls. Everything checked out this morning. Are you familiar with Praxx aircars?"

"Of course. I own several."

Berke nodded. "Just park it in the hotel lot when you're done. We'll have someone pick it up tomorrow."

"Thanks."

"No problem, sir. Thank you for using Teague Luxury Aircars, the best on Archaria III. Enjoy your trip." It sounded like a well-rehearsed script.

Solomon didn't waste any time. He climbed in, took the controls manually, and lifted off. The engine purred. The computer came on-line automatically as soon as he cleared the hotel's roof.

"Destination, sir?" it asked in its richly timbered Praxx voice.

Solomon released the controls. "Archo City Library, 5562 Vista Place." He had stationed the first of his fifty atmospheric monitoring stations there, on the rooftop.

"Very good, sir." The aircar banked to the left and began to accelerate. *"We will arrive in approximately five minutes."*

Solomon leaned back in his soft padded chair, which began to vibrate faintly, massaging his muscles. *Ah. Nothing like a Praxx vehicle,* he thought.

"Watch for aircars following us. If anyone takes a parallel course, inform me immediately."

"Of course, sir."

Solomon turned his head to gaze out the window. Nobody had reason to suspect him of any unlawful activities, of course, but with so few aircars out and about tonight, he knew he might catch some unwanted attention.

To the far north, he spotted a couple of official-looking troop transports flying quickly toward the spaceport. People could be so foolish, he thought, shaking his head. In a real plague situation, the *last* place you'd find him would be in a crowded public place. And yet half the planet seemed to be at the Archo City spaceport, trying desperately to get passage off Archaria III.

That very morning, he had watched a live broadcast from the spaceport terminal—the vid showed scenes of utter chaos, with flight counters closed, screaming masses of humans and Peladians fighting for space in nonexistent lines, children shrieking, mothers crying, fathers and brothers and cousins all on the verge of murder. And all just to escape a plague which couldn't possibly infect them.

Humans are crazy, he decided, and not for the first time in his life. The Peladians didn't seem much better.

"Hundreds of mixers trying to flee the planet have been collapsing in the spaceport terminal," the vid reporter said. *"Peace officers cart them off to a makeshift hospital as fast as they fall. Too bad they can't die at home."*

The makeshift hospital turned out to be a requisitioned circus tent erected on the landing pads between two parked starships. The vid showed a bright red-and-yellow striped tent as tall as the largest freighter, with dragon-shaped pennants fluttering from every peak and pinnacle. It looked ridiculous.

"That's right, Bob. With so many full-blooded

*humans here, the peace officers have enough prob-
lems keeping order without having to bother with
mixer trash—"*

Solomon shook his head. *Utter stupidity!* He
thought. They all, human and Peladians alike,
needed to go home and wait it out. With all off-
world traffic halted by the Federation, nobody
would be leaving Archaria III anytime soon . . .
not until the plague ran its course and burned itself
out, or somebody found a cure, whichever came
first.

He knew a cure wouldn't be long in coming. The
General had a whole timetable set up around the
plague. If events unfolded according to schedule,
the Federation would find a cure for the plague
virus within three weeks of their arrival here . . .
but only after 98 percent of the planet's half-breed
population were dead.

Solomon still had no idea *why* the General
wanted to kill off so many innocent people. Not
that it was his problem. But secretly, he half-
wished the Federation would find the cure a little
faster. He might be a member of the largest criminal organization in human space, but he didn't
consider himself a murderer. *And that's what this
is,* he thought. *Cold, calculated murder.*

He coughed a bit and fought a half-second of
panic. But the General wouldn't have infected him.
*He's not done with me yet. Phase Two has just
begun. He still needs my reports.*

The aircar circled down toward the roof of a
giant building complex: the Archo City Library. Its

roof held parking spaces for hundreds of vehicles. Now, however, it lay completely deserted.

"This is your destination, sir," the aircar told him. It began landing procedures, flashing bright yellow lights and sounding an insistent beep to alert anyone who might be directly underneath them. *"Will you be staying here long, sir? If so, I can power down and recharge my energy cells."*

"No, not long." He leaned to the side and studied the hundreds of empty parking spaces on the library's roof. *It must be closed for the emergency,* he thought. It was probably just as well. He didn't want anyone to see him checking his monitoring stations. Though that was hardly an illegal activity, he never liked explaining himself to strangers . . . or peace officers.

His aircar landed beside the lift.

"Thank you for using Teague Luxury Aircars, the best on the planet. Please enjoy your stay."

"I'll be back in just a second," he said. "Keep the engines fully powered up."

"Of course, sir."

Solomon popped open the side door, hopped out, and hurried to the lift. It looked like a small square building with double doors. The doors didn't open for him this time as he approached, not that it mattered—he had no intentions of going inside.

He went around to the back of the structure. A week ago he had installed an atmospheric monitoring station here. It was a small innocuous-looking silver box about the side of a small loaf of bread. Vents on all three exposed sides allowed air to pass through freely.

Pulling a small tricorder from his pocket, he snapped it into a data port on the front of the station. A red light turned green as the tricorder downloaded all the data.

Easy enough. Tucking the tricorder back into his pocket, he jogged back to the Praxx aircar. *One down, forty-nine more to go,* he thought. He would be lucky to finish by midnight.

He didn't know what atmospheric conditions the General's scientists needed to monitor, but then he didn't need to. *As long as they get their data and I get my pay, we'll all be happy.*

As he slid back into the pilot's seat, the computer said, *"Thank you for using Teague Luxury Aircars, the best on Archaria III!"*

Solomon rolled his eyes. *Forty-nine more monitoring stations . . . that message is going to get* very *annoying,* he thought.

"What is your next destination, sir?"

"225 Altair Place, Convent Gardens." He had a monitoring station set up amid the tangle of purple rosebushes along the Rose Walk.

Chapter Eleven

Dusk falls below. *The magic hour is here.*

In his cabin, Commander Riker stroked his long black beard and stared at himself in the mirror. He had never worn a beard before, and he had to admit he rather liked the effect. The follicle stimulator had given him a bushy growth in the style on a native Archarian. When he shrugged on a loose-fitting brown shirt and laced it up the front, then brown pants and soft brown boots, he barely recognized himself.

"Well, let's get going," he told himself.

He strode to the door and out into the corridor. Several crewmen did a double-take. Grinning, he nodded to them and said, "Carry on!"

"Sir." Data's voice came from behind, and Riker

paused long enough for the android to catch up. Data too wore loose brown clothing and sported a thick brown beard. Flesh-colored makeup hid the metallic gold of his face and hands; only his slitted yellow eyes still marked him as other than human.

"Your eyes—"

"I have inserts to change their color and appearance, sir. However, since they impair my vision by 1.0037 percent, I have elected not to wear them until we actually beam down to the planet."

Riker nodded. "Other than that, you look good, Data. Truly human . . . and ready to rebel."

"Thank you, sir. You also look substantially different."

"I'll take that as a compliment."

"That is how I intended it, sir."

They reached the turbolift, which hissed open promptly. Deanna Troi stood inside. She stared at them, then broke out in giggles. *That better not be the reaction we get on the planet,* Riker thought. He stepped inside, folded his arms and gave her a long stare. Oddly, her giggles grew louder, but at least this time she tried to stifle them a bit.

"Transporter Room Three," he said.

"Bill—" Deanna gasped. "You should see yourself!"

"I rather liked the effect." He stroked his beard and struck a new and even more heroic pose, one arm curled up and back with the first against his forehead. "I am a true planetary pioneer!"

"Sir," said Data, "very few human space pioneers actually wore beards. A comprehensive analysis starting with John Glenn in the mid-twentieth century shows—"

"Uh, that's not really what I meant, Data," said Riker.

"I'll leave you two to sort it out," Deanna said as the turbolift came to a stop. The doors shushed open and she stepped into the corridor, probably heading toward sickbay, Riker thought. She added over her shoulder, "Don't get too carried away, Bill."

"Thanks, Deanna—I think!" Riker called after her.

"May I ask you a question, sir?" Data said as the turbolift resumed its ascent.

"Certainly."

"Why does Counselor Troi call you 'Bill' when the rest of your fellow officers call you 'Will'?"

"I've known Deanna quite a bit longer than anyone else aboard. I used to go by Bill at the Academy—but then I dated a woman named Bili Beller, so we mutually decided I'd use Will." That conjured up images of her in his mind—tall and slender Bili, with her sea-green eyes, full pouting lips, and high cheekbones. He sighed and wondered what had happened to her.

He found Data staring inquiringly at him, so he cleared his throat and added, "Bill Riker and Bili Beller doesn't have the proper sound for a couple, so I went by Will. After we went our separate ways, I decided I liked Will better."

"The difference between two consonants seems inconsequential. Surely the measure of a man is determined by his actions, not his designation."

"Yes—and no. In some situations, the right name *can* make all the difference."

"And Will Riker is preferable to Bill Riker?"

"Or Billy-the-Kid Riker, a nickname I was also unfortunate enough to get stuck with at the Academy. So I had another reason to change it besides my girlfriend Bili."

Slowly Data nodded. "I believe I do see, sir. It is the difference between a shark and spark. Or a joke and a poke. Or a rose and a nose. Or—"

"Yes, exactly, Data."

"Is there a reason why you have not yet told Counselor Troi your new preference?"

"I, ah, haven't had a chance." *How do you tactfully explain the awkwardness of working with an old lover to an android?*

They reached the transporter room. As the doors slid open, Riker was pleased to find Lieutenant Yar already present. She, too, wore brown pants and shirt, but with a hooded cape slung almost casually across her shoulders. And like him, she had used a follicle stimulator; her suddenly long blond hair had been pulled back into a severe bun that accentuated the sharp lines of her jaw, cheekbones, and nose. She also wore no makeup . . . plain as a churchmouse, wasn't that the old saying? It fit this throwback racist zealot planet.

Yar turned to face him with a noticeable stiffening of her spine. *A month on board together and she hasn't relaxed once in my presence,* Riker thought. He had never seen anyone wound up so tight. *With the probable exception of Data. And with him it really is clockwork that's wound so tight.*

"Sir," Yar said. "I have your weapon. And Data's." She held out her left hand, revealing two small, gray, egg-shaped phasers of a design fit for civilians.

Riker and Data each accepted one. Riker turned his over, noting all the standard controls—pushbutton trigger, safety switch, and three degree settings—low, medium, and high. They would correspond to light stun, heavy stun, and kill, he knew. The lightly indented grips felt slightly different from standard Federation issue, as he wrapped his fingers around them . . . oddly soft and yielding, but still comfortable. He knew he could use the weapon with no difficulty.

The first rule of any away mission—drummed into every student at Starfleet Academy from day one—was to check your equipment personally. The phaser control had been set on light stun. When he tried to thumb it over to a higher setting, the switch jumped back. He thumbed it again with the same result.

"It's defective, Lieutenant," he said, offering it to her.

"No, sir," she said. "It's not unusual for civilians to bear arms on Archaria III, but local laws stipulate that any setting higher than 'light stun' must be permanently disabled on any weapon in civilian hands."

Riker nodded. "Have you selected a beamdown site?"

"Yes, sir. It's a small alley near Archo City Hospital. Civilian news broadcasts show an anti-mixer rally taking place there. It should start with speeches, chants, and the consumption of a lot of free alcoholic beverages. After that, it's anyone's guess—previous rallies have ended in everything from riots to lynch mobs chasing down mixers. Of course, a few have also ended peacefully." She grinned and he saw a little bit of a mischievous gleam in her eye. It was good to see her loosen up. "But that's not very likely tonight, from what I hear. Father Veritas wants Archo City Hospital destroyed, so I think we can pretty much count on some action."

Riker gave a nod. "Let's get moving," he said. He led the way onto the transporter platform, and Data and Yar took their positions to either side.

"Just a second, sir." Yar pulled up her hood and fastened a small silver chain under her chin. With her face suddenly hidden in shadow, only the faint glint of her icy blue eyes seemed alive. "It's traditional for Archarian woman to wear hoods in public," she said as if in reply to his scrutiny.

Data bent at the waist and pressed something to his face. When he rose, eyes as blue as Tasha Yar's met Riker's own. Riker blinked in sudden amazement. He would never have been able to pick Data out of a crowd of strangers. Not a single trace of the android's usual appearance remained.

"You would fool even your own mother, Data,"

he said in surprise. He gave a nod to Ensign Norman. "Energize!"

"Actually, sir," Data began, "I have no mother. Nevertheless, I view Dr. Soo—"

The transporter room shimmered, disappeared, and suddenly Riker found himself standing in a dark alley. The stench of decaying vegetation, raw sewage, old smoke, and several other even less savory smells hit him like a blow. Gagging, he steadied himself against a red-brick wall. Slowly his eyes grew accustomed to the dimness.

What little light spilled in from the streetlights in the street at the other end of the alley revealed nothing more than the vague outlines of abandoned crates and garbage bins around him. Every now and then humans passed the alley's mouth without so much as a glance in their direction, their silhouettes giving little clue about who they were and what they were up to. *Probably too busy hurrying away from the alley's stench,* Riker thought wryly.

"Yar, take point," he said.

"On it, sir." She glided up the alley as furtively as a shadow. If she hadn't been silhouetted against the light, he never would have seen her.

Riker started after her, but slipped on something slick and skated forward, off balance. Strong hands seized his shoulders and steadied him.

It was Data. "Careful, sir," the android said. "The ground offers little traction here."

"Thanks, Data."

"Actually, sir, given your thoughts on the matter,

I have been reconsidering my name. It conveys a sense of information rather than purpose. It is also not a name commonly associated with Acharians."

"Or humans."

"Precisely. Which is why I thought taking the name Bret might be a better choice—at least for the duration of this mission."

"Bret?" Riker shook his head a little. "How did you pick that one—no, never mind. I'm sure it's a well-researched and thought-out selection."

Data tilted his head slightly. "Thank you, sir."

"And you had better call me Will from now on, too. First names for everyone, like we're old friends out for fun at the Purity League rally."

"Acknowledged—Will."

Tasha Yar had reached the mouth of the alley. She paused and looked back, motioning them forward. Riker hurried to join her, with Data at his heels.

"Sir," she said softly, "there are peace officers posted at the both intersections to our left and right. I don't think we can get out without being seen."

Riker peeked out and spotted the two uniformed officers. Both stood beneath spotlights, looking conspicuous. *Probably what they want . . . an obvious authority presence to deter rioters and looters.* The planet wasn't under martial law yet, but the government had to be getting close to station peace officers so blatantly.

Yar went on, "There is still some pedestrian

traffic—I spotted a couple of people who looked like they might be factory workers hurrying home. The peace officers didn't even glance at them."

Riker said, "I don't think we'll have any trouble getting past them as long as we act like we belong here. Follow my lead. We'll bluff it through."

He took a deep breath and stepped out into the street with a little bit of a swagger, like he owned Archo City. With his beard and native garb, he knew he more than looked the part. To any casual observer, he *was* an Archarian.

Without hesitation Data and Yar joined him and matched his pace. *Just three friends out for an evening's fun at the Purity League rally,* Riker thought as they headed up the broad sidewalk. *We belong here. No need to question us.*

Yar said, "If my directions are correct, we need to turn right at the next intersection. Archo City Hospital is only a few blocks away."

"Excellent," Riker said. More loudly, he went on, "I think our harvest *will* be up ten percent this quarter."

"What harvest, Will?" Data said, sounding bewildered.

"Act like you belong here, Data!" Yar whispered fiercely at him. "Talk about farm stuff as we walk past the peace officers! Something innocuous!"

Data nodded woodenly, and suddenly he plastered a fake grin across his face. "Very well, Tasha," he said. "Since we are up to nothing more than business as usual, this seems like the perfect opportunity for me to practice humorous banter."

"Lucky for us it's dark!" Riker muttered half to himself. Data stood out like a Cardassian in Starfleet Headquarters when he tried too hard to be human.

"Will?" Data paused a millisecond, then went on, "So the farmer's daughter said to the traveling salesman—"

"Sorry, Bret, I've heard that one," Riker said.

"Bret?" Yar asked. "Did I miss something, sir?"

Riker sighed. "Long story, Tasha. In the alley, Bret here persuaded me that we should only use first names for the duration of the mission. Bret blends in better than Data. Proceed with your banter, Bret."

"Thank you, Will." Data paused a millisecond. "How about the one—"

"Heard it," Tasha said flatly.

Data frowned. "But how can you say you have heard it if I have not yet had a chance to relate the humorous part of the story?"

"I'll explain later," Riker told him.

They neared the intersection. Like all the other men on this planet, the peace officer waiting there wore his beard at chest length. He straightened a bit, looked them up and down, then started toward them at an amble.

Riker felt a jolt of panic and tried not to show it. *He's suspicious. What have we done wrong?*

His thoughts raced through the possibilities, and he studied his team from the corner of his eyes, but both Data and Tasha Yar looked the part of natives.

Feigning indifference, they kept strolling toward the corner. To all appearances they *were* three Archarians out for a walk. *So why is he heading our way?*

"Hey!" the peace officer called. "Hold up there. Wait a second!"

Riker stopped and turned reluctantly to face him. The man wore a black one-piece uniform with bulging pockets at the hips, thighs, and chest. In one hand he carried an old-fashioned billy club; clipped to his belt were a phaser, an old-fashioned communicator, and several other objects which Riker could not readily identify.

"Yes, officer?" Riker called. He felt a rush of adrenaline. *Fight or flight,* he thought, but he shoved those instincts to the back of his mind. They hadn't done anything wrong; they had no reason to be concerned.

"Do you want me to stun him, sir—Will?" Yar subvocalized. Casually she eased one hand toward her concealed phaser. "If we can get him into the alley before the other officer notices—"

"Let's see what he wants first," Riker replied. "Maybe we can talk our way through it. Volunteer no information."

"Yes, sir. Will."

Reaching them, the peace officer drew to a halt and said, "Father Veritas be with you, friends."

Was he a member of the Purity League? Or an overly diligent officer trying to trap them into a confession? *Better to play it cautiously,* Riker thought. *Father Veritas hasn't done anything illegal here. At least, not that we know of. There's no reason not to respond in kind.*

"And with you," Riker said. "Are you a member?"

"Of course I belong. Don't let the uniform fool you." He stuck out his hand. "Kirk Jordan."

"Will Riker." They shook briefly. Riker turned to Yar and Data. "These are a couple of my friends—Bret and Tasha."

Jordan gave them both nods. "Going to the rally?" he asked.

"Yes. We got a little held up."

"They've already started." Jordan seemed to be accepting their story at face value, Riker thought. The peace officer went on, "You're a bit turned about. Archo City Hospital's that way." He pointed to the right.

"Really?" Pointedly Riker glanced the way they had been headed and feigned surprise. "But I thought—"

"Nope." Jordan turned and pointed to the corner. "Turn right and then head straight. You can't miss it. And if you do get lost, just ask one of us. Peace officers *are* here to help, after all!"

Riker forced a grin. "Thanks!" he said. *No wonder the planetary government can't get a handle on their Purity League problem,* he thought. *The peace officers are part of it.*

Jordan grinned back. "Have fun. I only wish I could join you, but I pulled crowd control tonight."

"That's a shame," Tasha said. "I heard Father Veritas might actually speak tonight."

"Don't count on it. That's what the rumors always say before a big rally, but nobody *I* know has ever laid eyes on the Father." With a quick wave, he jogged back to his post. "Have fun!" he shouted over his shoulder. "Death to mixers! Humans first and always!"

"Humans first!" Riker echoed. If this was the sort of reception the Purity League gave newcomers, it looked more and more like they would have no trouble fitting in. He turned back to Yar and Data. "Let's go!"

Chapter Twelve

THIS TIME, IT WAS Dr. Tang who called *her*.

He must be starting to panic, Dr. Crusher thought. *I'm getting close to a cure, and now he's running scared. He knows he's going to be exposed.*

This time, though, she kept him waiting on the comm channel long enough to call Deanna Troi into the room, too. When she slid behind her desk and faced Tang, Deanna stood beside her, watching and evaluating.

"What can I do for you, Doctor?" she asked, using her best poker face. *One hundred percent virus-free!* she thought. Every test on her patient checked out perfectly. *We have a cure. And now we're going to catch you in your lies.*

"I had hoped to get a status update on the patient you sent through the biofilters."

"Well, I have good news. Our patient is cured."

He raised his eyebrows. "Completely? Are you sure?"

"It's been four hours since we beamed her through our modified biofilters, and we have run every test ever devised on her. She passed them all with flying colors. The virus is gone. She's well."

Tang nodded. "That is what I feared. I *knew* it would appear successful. However, it's too soon to judge."

"Doctor," she said, "this is getting silly. The virus is *gone*. The symptoms have disappeared. If she weren't still sedated, our patient would be up and dancing a jig. I don't know how much healthier she needs to be to prove she's cured."

Tang folded his arms stubbornly. "We had the same initial success with our own experiments with biofilters. Unfortunately, the disease always returned within twenty-four hours . . . it returned—and it was nastier than ever."

"It must have been reinfection."

"We thought so at first . . . but it happened even in clean rooms set up with level-1 containment fields. The same containment fields you are using."

"That's not possible. There is no way for anything as big as that virus to get through a containment field."

"Nevertheless," Tang insisted, "you must monitor the patient for at least two days before making any such rash claims of a cure. We don't want to raise false hopes. Check my reports. I documented everything that happened in my biofilter experiments in excruciating detail. No, Doctor." Tang shook his head firmly. "As much as I want to believe in your cure, based on my *significantly* greater experience with the disease you must maintain that quarantine for at least forty-eight more hours. If the disease does not returned within that period, I will be the first one to celebrate."

That did it. Dr. Crusher felt her professional resolve melt in a white hot fury.

"Listen to me!" she snapped. "I don't know what kind of game you're trying to pull, Tang, but I'm sick of it!"

He blinked in surprise. "What the—"

"I know you're behind the virus," she said. "You designed it for your Purity League friends, didn't you? That's why you're trying to block everyone else's research. Well, it's not going to work! It's just Rhulian flu with a few extra kinks—and not only have we cured *our* patient, we're going to have a vaccine within the day!"

"You're mad!" he said, staring at her with a horrified expression. "How—how can you even *think* that of me?"

"Then you deny it?"

"Yes—yes, absolutely!" He was almost speechless.

Dr. Crusher glanced up at Deanna Troi, who hesitated. *She's not sure. I have to push him further.*

"Knock it off, Tang," she said coldly. "Do yourself a favor and confess. If you turn over your research notes and the cure, maybe the courts will go easier on you."

"Doctor," he said urgently. "You are *wrong*. Everything in my notes *is* the truth. I would kill myself before taking another human life!"

"He's telling the truth," Deanna said suddenly.

"What?" Dr. Crusher took a deep breath. She felt as if her legs had just been kicked out from under her. She would have staked her job on Tang's guilt.

The sounds of a muffled explosion carried over the connection, and the room behind Dr. Tang seemed to shake. Dust sifted down from the ceiling and Tang steadied himself against the comm unit.

"What's going on down there, Doctor?" Deanna demanded. "Are you under attack? Do you need assistance?"

"The hospital has been under periodic attack for almost two weeks now. Every few hours someone lobs a grenade at our front door. We have force-fields up. Nobody can get inside if we don't want them to."

"That's horrible!"

"The Purity League wants my hospital burned, to 'purify' the diseased mixers inside. I get dozens of death threats every day—I don't dare leave the hospital anymore. Does that sound like the life of someone working *for* the Purity League?"

"No," Dr. Crusher said. She looked at Deanna Troi again.

"Yes, I really am sure," Deanna said in answer to her unasked question. "He is on the verge of a nervous breakdown. He is under incredible stress.

139

And he is innocent of everything you accused him of."

Tang was staring at her. "Who are you?" he demanded.

"I am the ship's counselor," she said. "Deanna Troi. I am pleased to meet you, sir."

"You're Betazoid—"

"Half Betazoid."

He swallowed. "Then you're going to be susceptible to the virus."

"I am . . . prepared to face that possibility."

"Ah." He blinked at them. "Ah, yes, I think I understand now. You two confronted me deliberately—you had to raise the possibility of my involvement with the Purity League to gauge my reaction, just in case I *was* involved."

"That's right," Dr. Crusher said. *I really put my foot in my mouth this time,* she thought with embarrassment. *At least I've got an out he can accept.* "Please—allow me to extend my apologies—"

"It is not necessary, I assure you. If I *had* been guilty, I'm sure I would have confessed!"

Dr. Crusher relaxed. *At least he isn't going to hold it against me,* she thought. She said, "About those attacks—are your patients safe?"

"Fortunately our security measures are more than capable, and the governor has troops posted at all entrances, so the truly needy can always get inside." He said it so matter-of-factly Dr. Crusher could scarcely believe it—Tang *accepted* a state of siege as the status quo.

"Do you need *any* assistance at all?" Deanna said. "I'm sure Captain Picard would beam down security forces to protect a hospital—"

"Not necessary. Our peace officers will suffice. And I do not wish to expose any of your crew to the dangers of infection. Now, if you'll excuse me, Doctor and Counselor, I have to work on finding a *real* cure."

How swiftly he took control of the conversation again and put her work down, Dr. Crusher thought. She found her teeth grinding in frustration, as Dr. Tang severed the link.

Incompetent, arrogant fool! she thought. *I have a patient cured here, and he won't even admit it!*

Deanna patted her shoulder. "If it helps, he really *does* think he's right. You might want to follow his advice about that woman—just in case."

Chapter Thirteen

JEAN-LUC PICARD ARRIVED at the transporter room just in time to see Captain Jules van Osterlich and two of his senior staff beam aboard. Jules had changed little in the three years since they had last seen each other . . . hair a little thinner, paunch a little bigger, but otherwise the same old friend from their days together at the Academy.

"Jules!" Picard said, stepping forward with a grin.

"Jean-Luc! You old spacedog!" Van Osterlich had been calling him that for the last thirty years.

They clasped arms and pounded each other on the back. It felt good to see Jules again, Picard thought. Command was often a lonely position, and he had learned to cherish his old friends all the more because of it.

"I'd like you to meet my senior officers," van Osterlich said. "This is Solack, my first officer—" Solack was a reed-thin Vulcan of perhaps eighty years . . . for a Vulcan, still in the prime of life. Solack inclined his head slightly in greeting. "—and Dr. Benjamin Spencer. Benny is my chief medical officer."

"Solack, Doctor." Picard gave them both polite nods. "I would like to give you a quick tour of our sickbay first, so Dr. Crusher can bring you up to date on her research."

"I would appreciate that, Captain," Dr. Spencer said.

Picard led the way out to the turbolift, trying to make polite small talk along the way. And yet he sensed something bothering his old friend. Jules seemed . . . distracted somehow. Not his usual self.

As they reached sickbay and the door whooshed open, Solack and Dr. Spencer went in first. Picard hooked his old friend's arm and held him back.

"What's bothering you?" he asked.

He licked his lips. "Jean-Luc . . . this whole set-up stinks. I know the plague is man-made. Benny and your Dr. Crusher have been comparing notes since we reached orbit, and I've seen the message written on it. I have a theory."

Picard folded his arms. "Let's hear it." Jules had an almost uncanny knack for putting his finger on the heart of any problem.

"I don't know who created the plague, but I'll

143

wager it wasn't done here or to the Purity League's order."

"Why not? Dr. Crusher suspects one of the staff at Archo City Hospital, a virologist named Tang. She's quite adamant about his guilt. He *has* been trying to hinder her research."

"I know. And she's wrong."

A pair of crewmen passed them, and Picard gave them a nod. Only when they were out of earshot did he turn back to his friend.

"Explain."

"I've known Ian Tang almost as long as I've known you. He's a good man, and he's 100 percent dedicated to his work . . . to healing. He would never be a party to mass murder!"

Picard frowned. "If so . . . then who *is* responsible?"

"I don't know yet. But I have a feeling sooner or later he'll tip his hand. You don't play games on a planetary scale unless something larger is at stake."

Picard nodded. "I agree. But until our culprit does reveal himself, we must proceed as though the virus is our sole concern. Let's see what progress Dr. Crusher has made."

They are still drinking, Worf thought with growing apprehension. From ahead came a new bout of boisterous Klingon song—a popular old drinking tune with a rousing chorus:

Comrades in death, in death we live!
Drink up my brothers, tomorrow we give!

Death to the humans! Death to our foe!
Death to the Romulans! Strike a deadly blow!

He knew it well. Legions of Klingon warriors had sung that song for more than a hundred years, drinking to victory in their wars with Earth and Romulus. On "blow" they would drain their tankards of blood wine, then slam them down.

From the way they slurred their words, Worf knew the celebration had been going on a long time . . . a very long time indeed. And there was nothing more dangerous than a drunken Klingon.

He paused and looked back at his three young ensigns. Knowing the dangers, he couldn't let them face these Klingons. They were too inexperienced. Look at how Wrenn had handled a few corpses.

"Stay back," he said. "I must face these Klingons alone."

"Alone, sir? But, Sir . . . " Clarke began.

Worf glared. "These are Klingons!" he said. "They are singing songs about killing humans and Romulans. Do not question my orders again."

"Yes sir. I mean, no sir," Clarke blushed.

Worf stopped listening.

Taking a deep breath, he turned and strode up to the open hatch, stuck his head inside, and saw all ten Klingons in various stages of drunkenness. They were lounging on chairs, benches, and the floor holding tankards aloft, singing at the top of their lungs. A large keg of blood wine sat before them . . . and it was more than half gone.

The singing trailed off as they began to notice him. Several fumbled for mek'leths. One—their leader?—staggered to his feet.

"Put down your weapons," Worf said in Klingon.

"You—you are Klingon!" their leader said, his words slurring.

Worf glared. "And you are a disgrace to our people!"

"I am Krot of the House of Mok! No one insults me!"

Worf took three quick steps forward and backhanded Krot across the face. The Klingon crashed back into a weather-monitoring station. The equipment sparked and died.

"I am Worf, son of Mogh!" he roared through his helmet, "and I serve aboard the Starfleet vessel *Enterprise!* You have violated Federation law. You have killed humans here. What do you have to say for yourselves?"

Krot staggered to his feet, grinning. "Worf? I have never heard of you . . . and a Klingon serving aboard a *Federation* ship? I spit on you and your house, you simpering would-be human!"

Worf backhanded him again, but this time Krot was ready. Shrugging off the blow, he punched Worf in the head with the full strength of a Klingon warrior.

Worf staggered. His faceplate had cracked a dozen ways, he saw. As he shook off the blow, Krot reached forward, snagged his helmet, and *pulled.*

The helmet came off with a tearing sound. The seals hadn't held—not that it really mattered after the faceplate had shattered.

Roaring in rage, Worf tried a head-butt. He caught Krot by surprise, and the Klingon leader reeled back, this time laughing like a demon. A thin line of blood ran from a cut over his left eye. Worf glared his rage.

"Join us, Worf!" Krot shouted. "Maybe you are a real Klingon!" He picked up a tankard, dipped it into the keg of blood wine, and held it out. "Drink up! Sing the old songs! Let us know what kind of warrior you are!"

What have I done? Worf thought. He had exposed himself to the plague virus. *I cannot return to the* Enterprise.

He swallowed. Somehow, the thought did not alarm him. *Perhaps that is what I wanted,* he thought. *To see my own kind. At least for a day or two, until Dr. Crusher finds her cure.*

He accepted the tankard from Krot and raised it high in the air. "To the Emperor!" he cried.

"To the Emperor!" the others roared. They chanted as he raised the tankard to his lips. He drained it in a few deep gulps, and when he slammed it down and wiped his mouth with the back of his arm, they cheered.

Chapter Fourteen

As Captain Picard entered sickbay, he paused in surprise. He had never seen it this busy before. Strange new equipment beeped or hummed on every workbench. Doctors, nurses, and scientists hustled around one another, carrying data padds, tricorders, and other devices. The bustle reminded him more of the training hospital at Starfleet Academy, with its dozen-interns-to-one-patient ratio. Dr. Crusher clearly had everyone working double or triple shifts. Every doctor, every nurse, and as far as he could tell every biologist aboard had been co-opted into the research.

And their case at hand . . . he took a moment to study the woman lying on the biobed in the middle of the room, the eye of the storm. A forcefield shimmered faintly around her. She had curiously smooth features and a slightly elongated skull, with wide dark eyes and pale skin. A flood of black hair spilled around her head. Despite being deathly ill, she had the sort of ethereal beauty of which poets speak.

"Doctor Crusher!" he called when he spotted Beverly on the far side of sickbay, examining microcellular readouts on the wall scanner. The machine bleeped as she entered new data. "May we see you for a minute."

She turned and noticed him. "Captain! And this must be Captain van Osterlich."

"That's right. I believe you already know Dr. Spencer, and this is Mr. Solack, the *Constitution*'s first officer. Gentlemen, may I present my chief medical officer, Dr. Beverly Crusher."

"I'm pleased to meet you." She turned toward the unconscious woman on the biobed. "We were just about to wake our test subject. She went through our transporter and a series of modified biofilters about five hours ago. We have been monitoring her condition, and I'm glad to report things look promising. The virus appears to be gone from her system."

"Do I hear a 'but'?" Picard asked.

"I'm afraid so. On Dr. Tang's advice, I am going to keep the containment field up and monitor her condition for another day or two to make absolutely sure."

Deanna Troi joined them, and once more Picard made the round of introductions.

"Have you told them yet?" Deanna asked Dr. Crusher.

"Told us what?" Picard demanded.

"Dr. Tang is innocent," Dr. Crusher said with a sigh. "I confronted him with Deanna present to monitor his reactions, and I'm afraid he passed. He isn't responsible for the disease."

Picard shot a glance at van Osterlich, who returned an I-told-you-so shrug.

"Go on," Picard told her. "You still don't look happy. Now that you know you can trust his data, I would think you would find him a valuable resource."

"That's the problem—his data are crazy! He insists the virus leaps level-one containment fields. And we all know that's impossible."

"Is it?" van Osterlich said. He glanced at his own chief medical officer. "Benny?"

"I'm afraid it sounds crazy to me, too. The containment field keeps out particulate matter. Its field's screen is set so fine that oxygen gets through but nothing else—no dust, no bacteria, no viri. Dr. Crusher has isolated the plague virus, and it's clearly a simple variation of Rhulian flu. It's simply *too large* to get through any containment field— you can't alter the laws of physics just because they're inconvenient!"

Dr. Crusher said, "Let me show you our patient." She led the way toward the biobed. "This is Jenni Dricks. She is one-quarter Peladian. We beamed her through that modified transporter field

I mentioned—using two sets of biofilters—and to all appearances it worked perfectly. Not a trace of the plague virus remains in her body. But that's only half the problem."

"Why?" Picard asked.

"We eliminated the virus from her body, but she's still going to be susceptible to it once she beams back down to the planet."

Solack raised one eyebrow. "She cannot go home."

"Not until a real cure is found. Nor can anyone leave the planet who might be carrying the virus. We haven't found a cure so much as . . . a delaying tactic. Of course, we can beam people up and pass them through biofilters, such as our away team, but with a planet as large as this one with a population in the millions, it's a task that will take years. And we still won't have eliminated the virus in the wild."

"But surely it's a good start," Picard said. As long as they could contain the disease, that would buy its victims time until a real cure could be found and they could return to their old lives.

Dr. Crusher shook her head. "Unfortunately, it's going to be a drop in the bucket, so to speak. There isn't room on the *Enterprise* to rescue more than a fraction of the plague victims. The latest estimates—and that's all Dr. Tang can give me at this point—indicate roughly thirty-five *thousand* people have died of the disease. Another twenty thousand are infected. It would take weeks to beam them all through our biofilters using both ships and working around the clock. And we don't have enough room here to house a *tenth* of that number, even if we use the shuttlebays and cargo holds."

"I see your point," Picard said. The situation truly was disastrous, he thought. "But at least we have some good news—with the biofilters working, we can come and go as necessary."

"But everyone who leaves the planet will still have to go through a quarantine period," Dr. Crusher said. "Just to make sure. Dr. Tang's data may be crazy, but I don't want to take any chances."

"Agreed." He turned to van Osterlich. "Are you ready for dinner? I have some other ideas I wish to discuss with you. And that Saurian brandy I promised!"

"Of course," van Osterlich said with a grin. "Lead the way, Jean-Luc!"

"If you don't mind," Dr. Spencer said, "I would prefer to remain here and work on the virus."

"And I should return to the *Constitution*," Solack said in a flat voice.

"Of course," van Osterlich said.

"This way," Picard said, heading for the door.

Deanna Troi crossed to Jenni's biobed and gazed at her through the shimmering forcefield. "You said you were going to wake her?"

"Yes, I think it's time. I no longer see any medical reason to keep her unconscious. The worst of the plague symptoms are gone."

Deanna turned to look at the patient on the biobed again. Up close, you could still see the ravages of the disease in the woman, Deanna thought. Small white scars covered her face and hands, but those would undoubtedly fade away in time. For someone who had been at death's door less than twelve hours ago, the change in her appearance could only be described as miraculous.

She reached out with her mind, feeling the turbulent emotions of a dreaming mind . . . a mix of fear and dread and horror. *Nightmares,* she realized.

"What can you tell me about her?"

"According to her file, Jenni is a quarter Peladian. Her husband was half-human, half-Peladian, and they had three children. Due to their genetic human-Peladian mix, all five proved highly susceptible to the plague."

"You're using the past tense. Is there something I should know?"

Dr. Crusher shrugged helplessly. "I don't know. I haven't been able to find out if the rest of her family is still alive. It's highly unlikely, since she was apparently the last of them to fall ill, and death counts are still rising rapidly all over the planet."

Deanna regarded the woman on the biobed. "Go ahead," she said. "I'll do what must be done."

Since Dr. Crusher could not reach through the containment field, she had the computer administer the stimulant directly through the biobed. In a few seconds, Jenni took a deep breath, opened her eyes, sat up—and screamed.

"It's all right," Deanna said soothingly. She felt the terror surging through their patient.

"Where am I?"

"You're on board the *Starship Enterprise*. You were fortunate enough to be a test subject—we are trying to cure the plague. And we think it worked on you."

"Then—I'm well?" She looked from face to face.

"That's right," Deanna said. "This is Dr. Crusher. She's the one who cured you."

"Hi, Jenni." Dr. Crusher smiled. "How do you feel?"

"Terrible—but much better!"

"Good."

"Jenni," Dr. Crusher said, "I'd like you to meet a friend. This is Deanna Troi, the ship's counselor. Deanna, this is Jenni Dricks."

"What about my children—my husband—" she asked.

"We don't know what happened to them," Deanna said. "The hospital record system has completely broken down."

"You have to find them—cure them, too—"

"We're working on it as fast as we can," Dr. Crusher said. "We hope to have a vaccine sometime tomorrow."

Jenni gave a sigh and sank back down. "They're dead," she said. Deanna felt despair come from her in waves.

"We don't know that—"

"I know it." She stared straight at the ceiling,

and as Deanna watched, a tear rolled down her cheek, then another. Her emotions turned dark with an almost suicidal undertone.

Deanna drew Dr. Crusher aside. "Are you sure you don't know anything?" she asked softly.

"I tried to locate them, but I haven't been able to find their records." Dr. Crusher shook her head. "The support system in the hospital has completely broken down. It's impossible to get any queries answered. I would have gotten them all beamed up here if I could have."

"I'll try to find out what happened, then. That's my job, and I know how busy you are." Deanna never liked being the bearer of tragic news, but sometimes it could not be helped. At least she could make a few calls down to the hospital.

She returned to the biobed. Jenni turned and regarded her through dark, half-closed eyes.

"I'm feeling well enough to get up," the woman said, and she managed a wan smile. "I'm ready to return home. Can you beam me back down to the hospital?"

"You're in no condition for that," Deanna said. "I will try to locate your family. Dr. Crusher says we can beam them up for treatment. You have to understand that the doctors on your planet are so overwhelmed with treating the plague that they've stopped keeping accurate records—everything except plague research. It's not as simple as looking up their names in the computer's database anymore."

She turned to Dr. Crusher again. "Beverly, can you release the containment forcefield yet? I feel awkward standing outside—especially since Jenni is cured."

Dr. Crusher said, "I'm afraid not. We have to keep that two-day quarantine to make sure you're really well."

Deanna dragged over a chair and sat. "I'm going to need to know the names of your other family members. I don't know how easy it's going to be, but I promise you this—I will do my best to find out where they are."

"Thank you." She sank back with a little shiver and her large brown eyes seemed to droop. "My husband is Derek Dricks. My children are Vera, Thomas, Jason, and David."

She just needed a little reassurance, Deanna thought. She sensed a rising contentment within Jenni. *Someone to take over the responsibility of finding things out. Now that it's my job, she can rest.*

She did not look forward to discovering the truth about Jenni's family. *She had to admit, their chances of survival were slim.* Telling someone their loved ones were gone had to be the hardest task for any ship's counselor. It was the one part of her job she truly hated.

But I don't really know, she told herself. *We delivered the Tricillin PDF ahead of schedule. They could be holding on. There's a chance it kept them alive.*

At least a slight chance.

She glanced at Dr. Crusher. *Beverly thinks they're dead.* Beyond the raw hurt coming from Jenni, she sensed Dr. Crusher's true feelings: regret, remorse, sadness, and a touch of wistful nostalgia for her own lost husband.

"I'll tell you what I'll do," Deanna said suddenly, trying to sound a little more cheerful. "I'll go now and see what I can find out. With any luck, I'll have word by midnight. Is that acceptable?"

"Yes, thank you." Jenni smiled.

"Try to get some sleep," Deanna said as she stood. She felt a faint rumble in her stomach. *But I just had dinner,* she thought. "I'll take care of everything. If I have news, I promise I'll wake you."

"You look pale," Jenni said as she sat up. Deanna could hear the sudden alarm in her voice. "Are you all right? *Are you all right?*"

"I should be asking you that ques—"

Deanna gasped soundlessly. What felt like the blade of a knife turned in her guts. The pain, as sharp and hot as a real wound, cut through her so fast she couldn't breathe. Unable to do more than gasp, she half doubled over, clutching her stomach.

Dr. Crusher steadied her arm. "What is it—Deanna?"

And just as suddenly as it started, the pain disappeared. Taking a deep shuddering breath, Deanna met the doctor's gaze.

"It's the plague—" Jenni wailed. She had a terrified expression on her face.

157

"Nonsense," Deanna said firmly. It simply wasn't possible. "I must have pulled a muscle. I had a strenuous workout on the holodeck just a couple of hours ago."

"Oh. For a second, I thought you had it, too!" Jenni sank back with a nervous laugh. Her face looked as white as chalk to Deanna.

"I think I'd better take a look at you, anyway," Dr. Crusher said. "Hop up on biobed two."

She felt another rumble in her intestines. *It's probably nothing—something I ate. Maybe the replicators are acting up . . .*

That had to be the solution.

She took a step, and suddenly sickbay wobbled and the deck seemed to slide out from under her feet. She felt herself falling and grabbed for an instrument tray. Clattering loudly, medical devices scattered across the floor, and she pitched after them, coming to rest against biobed 2.

"Ah-h-h-h-h!" she heard herself cry. It sounded like the death cry of a wounded animal.

New pains blossomed in her stomach. Molten steel burned through her veins, seared to the lengths of her arms and legs, shot down her spine, radiated from her bones.

The universe spun around her. The pain grew even worse. Lancets sliced through her bones. Fires coursed through her limbs. *Please, make it stop, make it stop!* She couldn't move, couldn't think—

Suddenly feet appeared in front of her eyes. Dr. Crusher rolled her onto her back. She had a medical tricorder in hand and Deanna heard its low whir.

"Deanna—Deanna—can you hear me?" Dr. Crusher demanded. She turned Deanna's face toward her own and skinned back her left eye, then her right.

She tried to talk but only a raw moan of pain came out.

And then, as suddenly as a door slamming shut, the pain vanished. Deanna lay there panting and soaked in sweat. *What's wrong with me?*

Her hands shook when she raised them to her face. Softly she began to sob. She had never felt anything so horrible, so excruciatingly painful, in her entire life.

"Deanna—talk to me!" Dr. Crusher pried her hands away from her face. "Tell me what's wrong!"

Deanna forced herself to meet the doctor's gaze. *What happened?* She wondered. *Was it a seizure?* Her teeth began to chatter. Dr. Crusher was staring at her with a half-terrified, half-worried expression. A cold wind swept through her body.

"S-so c-col—c-cold!" She felt her whole body begin to shake, and she couldn't stop no matter how hard she tried.

"Give me a hand! Get her on a biobed!" Dr. Crusher said to Dr. Spencer.

Together they seized Deanna's limbs, lifted on the count of three, and bustled her over to a biobed. Deanna gasped as new pains shot through her chest and stomach. She had never felt this sick before in her life—sick and out of control. She felt her eyes rolling back.

"Ahhhh-nahhh-hh—" she heard a distant voice cry. *It's me,* some part of her realized. *I'm starting to dissociate from my body.*

That only happened in severe traumas or in cases where the pain became too great for a patient to deal with rationally. *So the mind starts to float free, apart from the body, an observer to the terror within.*

She tried to relax as the two doctors set her down on the biobed. Her shaking grew worse. She couldn't breathe, couldn't think. Distantly, she felt them strapping down her arms and legs. No matter how hard she tried, she couldn't make her body cooperate. She felt helpless and panicked.

"It's the plague!" she heard Jenni wail from across the room. "That's how it starts! I saw it in my husband and children!" She began to weep hysterically.

Deanna tried to sit up as the pain faded again. *I ought to comfort her,* some part of her realized—but on second thought, she knew she was in no condition to do much of anything. She needed someone to comfort *her.*

"Quiet!" Dr. Crusher barked at Jenni over her shoulder. *The first rule of triage,* Deanna thought, *is to treat the most critically wounded. Hysterical but otherwise well patients get shoved to the rear of the line.*

"It can't be the plague!" Dr. Spencer said.

But it is! Deanna thought. *Somehow, some way, I have it.* She knew; she had read the reports. There couldn't be any mistaking these symptoms. *It leaped the containment field. Dr. Tang was right—*

She pressed her eyes shut as new pains welled up in her belly. *And there's no time for bedside manners,* she thought.

This time as the white-hot irons pierced her innards, she began to scream, and nothing could make her stop.

Dr. Crusher worked frantically. *It can't be the plague,* she told herself over and over, as she reconfigured the biobed for a half-Betazoid, half-human biology. *Her symptoms be damned, it's impossible.* Impossible! *Our plague victim is cured. She and Deanna weren't in direct contact. No virus moves through a containment field—*

Still Deanna screamed. Then her breath came in rapid pants—then suddenly she went limp, unconscious from the pain. *Best thing for her,* Dr. Crusher thought with dismay.

"Her fever is still climbing rapidly," Nurse Anders said urgently.

That was another one of the plague's first signs. *But it can't be,* Dr. Crusher thought. *There's no way she could possibly be infected.*

"Doctor?" the nurse asked.

"Almost done . . . there!" The biobed was reconfigured. It began its automatic scanning process. Charts began to appear: heart, respiration, blood pressure, white blood cell count.

As Dr. Crusher studied the readouts, her mouth went dry. *Viral infection. Similar to Rhulian flu.*

It can't be.

But there couldn't be any doubt—Deanna *was* infected with the plague virus. The green graph that mapped microorganism activity showed it multiplying at a dizzying rate. From the genetic signature, it couldn't be anything else *but* the plague.

But how? It was a medical impossibility. Nothing can get through a containment field. There must be another answer.

She exchanged a quick glance with Dr. Spencer. From their startled reaction, she knew he had reached the same conclusion.

"It's crazy. Just like Dr. Tang's report," she growled, her fists clenched in frustration.

"Maybe not so crazy," he said. "Maybe he missed something. Maybe *we* missed something."

"Back to basics. Contain and control."

"Exactly."

She glanced around sickbay. Everyone present— seventeen humans, a Vulcan, a Bolian—was of pure genetic heritage. *Good.* They wouldn't have anyone else dropping in the middle of their work.

"Staff meeting!" she called. They had all been watching; they knew what had happened. They all gathered around in record time.

"We must contain this outbreak," she said, meeting their gazes one by one. "We have all—every one of us in this room—been exposed to the plague virus. Chances are good we're carriers; however, it's not going to affect us. We're going to have to work under strict quarantine restrictions until we can assess the damage. Anders, seal the doors. Smith, draw a blood sample from Counselor Troi. Everyone else—keep working. We need to find that vaccine!"

Dr. Spencer touched her arm. "Our captains— and Mr. Solack!" he said with a groan.

She winced. They were loose on the ship—and Solack had beamed back to the *Constitution*. A disaster on all fronts.

"Call Solack," she told him. "Maybe it can still be contained on your ship. I'll take care of our captains."

"A toast—" Captain Picard said, raising his goblet. He heard a strange hum and paused. *Transporter beam*—he realized as he saw his hand dissolve in a shimmer of colored light.

And the next thing he knew, he stood in sickbay facing Dr. Crusher. She had her hands on her hips. Around her, the medical staff scrambled with panicked expressions.

"What the hell are you doing?" he demanded.

"Sorry, Captain," she said. "Time was pressing. Deanna has come down with the plague virus." She pointed to biobed 2.

Picard stared. *Her face*—it had broken out in what looked like small white pustules.

"That's impossible!" Captain van Osterlich said.

"But it happened. Did you come into contact with anyone on the way back to your cabin?"

"An ensign—Ensign Clarke, who wanted to see me about a complaint, and I put him off until tomorrow morning. And I introduced Lieutenant La Forge to Captain van Osterlich."

"And there was the Vulcan—"

"Yes, Ensign T'Pona. And we shared a turbolift with several people—the Praxx whose name I can't pronounce and Ensign Crane."

"Tr'grxl-gn'ta," Crusher said, naming the Praxx. "He's letting people call him Tray now."

"That's the one." He frowned. "I believe that's all."

Dr. Crusher shook her head. "Too many. Too damn many. We'll never get this genie stuffed back in the bottle." She glanced at Dr. Spencer, who was talking urgently to someone over the comm link in the corner. "Let's hope Spencer has better luck."

Van Osterlich paled. "Solack—"

"Beamed back to the *Constitution* as soon as you left," Dr. Crusher finished.

He sprinted to join Dr. Spencer, and the two of them held an animated conversation.

Picard began to pace. *How many crewmen are going to prove susceptible? How many people of mixed genetic heritage are actually serving onboard the* Enterprise?

Deanna stirred and moaned a bit. Picard trailed Dr. Crusher to her side and watched as she administered a sedative hypospray. *No need for containment fields now,* he thought. Small comfort.

"I've already given her a shot of Tricillin PDF," she said. "That will help."

Deanna settled down and lay quietly. *Rest. That's the best thing for her right now,* he thought. *Let the doctors do their work. They'll find a cure.*

Picard chewed his lip, thinking through the possibilities. He glanced at his friend.

"Jules?" he called.

Shaking his head, van Osterlich rejoined him. "They had a staff meeting in my absence," he said. "It seems they were going to hold a surprise party for one of my lieutenants. It's too late. Half the crew must have been exposed at this point."

Picard heard sobbing. He turned and found Dr. Crusher's original patient—the beautiful woman who had been asleep—now sitting up on her bed.

"What's wrong?" he asked her.

"It's my fault," she said. "I brought the plague here!"

"Nonsense," he said. "That wasn't your fault. We'll lick this thing yet."

"Hang on," Dr. Crusher said. She brought her medical tricorder over and began to run scans on her first patient. "How are you feeling?"

"Like I just had my stomach kicked." Her lower lip trembled.

"This is very interesting." Dr. Crusher raised her tricorder and began a second scan. "Very interesting indeed."

"What?" Picard asked.

"I'm picking up the virus in Jenni's blood . . . it's the very first stage of infection." She shut off the tricorder with a snap. "I don't think you've been infected longer than an hour. Which means you didn't infect Deanna—she infected *you*. Her case is at least eight hours old."

"How is that possible?" Picard demanded. "You were supposed to have a level-one containment field up around her at all times—"

"Yes, Captain, we did. We *still do*—nobody bothered to take it down."

Picard turned to look at Jenni. "It's still up . . . run a full diagnostic. It must be malfunctioning!"

"It's not. These events match what Dr. Tang told us. Somehow, somewhere, our quarantine procedure failed."

Think! Picard told himself. *That's the problem here—we're being outwitted. Whoever designed that virus is laughing at us. What have we missed?*

This wasn't like any other virus humanity had ever encountered, despite its resemblance to Rhulian flu.

Nurse Anders ran up. "Doctor," she said urgently. "We have two more suspected cases of the plague. They're on their way to sickbay now. Shall we lift the quarantine on sickbay?"

Two more cases . . . that confirmed it, Picard thought. Deanna Troi had been spreading the virus through the ship all day.

"Yes," he said. "Speed is of necessity here. Have a site-to-site transport beam them directly here."

"Get them started on Tricillin PDF," Dr. Crusher said. "That's about all we can do right now."

"Yes, Doctor."

Turning, Picard studied Deanna's readouts. Her

vital signs appeared to have stabilized, at least for the moment.

"We can't look at this as a tragedy," Dr. Crusher said. "Three more plague victims means three more test subjects . . . and a better chance of finding a cure."

"That's the attitude," Picard said. Never mind that the plague was loose on the *Enterprise*.

Chapter Fifteen

PEACE OFFICER JORDAN'S DIRECTIONS proved
unnecessary—you would have had to be blind
and deaf to miss the demonstration going on,
Riker thought.

PEACE OFFICER JORDAN'S DIRECTIONS proved
unnecessary—you would have had to be blind
and deaf to miss the demonstration going on,
Riker thought.

The noise reached deafening levels from three
blocks away. As they followed the chanting,
shouting, screaming, and out-and-out war-whoops
to their source, they came to a broad parklike
square where five streets came together. In the
center of the square, atop a small grassy knoll,
blazed a huge bonfire. Hundreds had gathered
around it chanting *"Veritas! . . . Veritas! . . .
Veritas!"* Others screamed antimixer slogans,
waved angry fists at the hospital complex on the
far side of the bonfire, or just talked, shouted, or
jeered, all at the top of their lungs. The noise

reached deafening levels. Riker began to worry about damage to their eardrums.

Tasha touched his arm and pointed, mouthing, "The hospital!"

He nodded and began to follow her as she picked her way through the crowds of revelers. They passed more uniformed peace officers, none of whom looked happy. *They're missing the party,* Riker realized. *They're all members of the Purity League, or Purity League sympathizers . . . wolves watching the sheep.* Hopefully whatever oaths they had sworn to do their duty will keep them in line . . . *They would rather join in than keep the peace.* Not that there was much peace to keep in this bedlam.

Men and women gave him friendly nods and waves and pats on the back, and he reciprocated. *Look like you're having fun,* he thought. *Blend in. We're all one big family here, united in our fear and paranoia.*

Reaching the fringes of the crowd, Lieutenant Yar circled slowly to the left. A couple of people gave her too-friendly slaps on the back and shoulder and rump, and he could tell it took all her restraint to keep from breaking their arms. Here he could see open kegs of liquor—people were passing cups of it everywhere.

Yar turned and shouted something he couldn't quite make out over the thunderous tumult around them. He shrugged helplessly and pointed to his ears. She nodded, accepted a couple of cups of liquor from one of the Purity Leaguers, and handed him one. Data, too, took one—*That's right,* Riker thought, *he's capable of eating and drinking. Practically human in every way physically.* Though of course Data couldn't metabolize food—he would eject it later.

Following the lead of the men around him, Riker raised one fist in the air and began to shout. Of course, nobody could hear him. Data and Yar began to shout, too—and to Riker's eye they all looked like dutiful members of the League.

Slowly they began to work their way around toward the far side of the bonfire, closer to Archo Hospital. Riker had a feeling, somehow, that when violence erupted, it would be in that direction. He wanted them . . . if not in the middle of it, at least close enough for firsthand observation.

At one point Riker turned to Data and mouthed: "How many people are here?"

Data used his fingers to flash a quick number: 5-5-0-0. *Fifty-five hundred.* Riker had estimated three or four thousand, but Data's number had to be closer to the truth. The android could count samples and extrapolate far better than he could.

On the far side of the bonfire they found a crude wooden platform already set up before the entrance of the Archo Hospital complex. A few men stood on the platform, shouting slogans he couldn't hear and periodically pointing at the line of six bored-looking peace officers who stood on the hospital's steps. The peace officers all wore riot gear, complete with shields, masks, and billy clubs.

"I thought you said this was going to be a riot!" he said slowly to Tasha, mouthing the words carefully so she could read his lips. It wasn't so much a riot as a boisterous demonstration, he decided. The six peace officers could be overwhelmed in seconds if a crowd this size turned violent.

"Wait!" she answered. "It will get worse!"

Riker turned his attention back to the platform. It seemed to be the center of protest activity. In front of it, several dozen men and women passed out pamphlets, flyers, and even banner signs with antimixer slogans printed on them:

ARCHARIA IS FOR HUMANS
WE WELCOME THE PLAGUE!
DEATH TO MIXERS

These had to be the demonstration's organizers . . . or at least a step closer to them. Riker approached, and a girl of perhaps sixteen pressed a flyer into his hands, smiling broadly at him. A redheaded young man with a full red beard pressed a banner on him—"Better Dead Than Impure!" He motioned for Riker to wave it.

171

Riker handed the sign to Data and turned back, but the girl and the redheaded man had moved on. He started for the platform, hoping to find someone in charge . . . when suddenly a bell began to toll.

The clear ringing tone cut through the noise of the demonstration. Everyone froze for a second, and between peals Riker could hear the crackle and hiss of the giant bonfire. The whole crowd seemed to be holding its breath in anticipation. Everyone began to turn toward the platform.

Spotlights went on, illuminating the stage in a soft, warm glow. Slowly, carefully, an old man in white robes climbed the steps to stand before them. He had to be seventy or eighty years old, Riker thought, and his steel-gray beard stretched nearly to his waist. Could this be the mysterious Father Veritas? Could this really be the secretive leader of the Purity League? Riker felt his pulse quicken.

A whispering sound came from the multitude: "Father Veritas!" most of them seemed to be saying.

"Friends." The old man's voice held a slight quaver, but it still boomed across the square— amplified by some hidden speaker system, Riker assumed. *"Friends, I am Brother Paul, a close friend of Father Veritas. Tonight I bring you a message from the Father himself. He bids me to thank you all for your support. The day of human freedom is at hand. Death to mixers!"*

"Freedom is ours!" the crowd shouted back.

So this wasn't Father Veritas, Riker thought, but one of his inner circle, sent out to speak the gospel to the multitudes.

"Are you with the League?" Brother Paul demanded.

"Freedom is ours!" the crowd roared.

"Do you love your freedom?"

"Freedom is ours!" the crowd roared again.

"Will you follow the Father to pure human salvation?"

"Freedom is ours!" the crowd screamed. *"Death to mixers! Death to mixers! Death to mixers!"*

Riker thought it sounded like a litany—everyone around them seemed to expect the questions and know the proper response. The Purity League certainly had draped itself in the trappings of a religion, he decided . . . complete with Fathers and Brothers.

"You know what must be done!" Brother Paul shouted. *"Now is the time for human freedom! Now! Now! Now!"*

Cheering, the crowd rushed the hospital's front steps. The peace officers holding the riot gear—all smirking with ill-concealed glee—simply stepped aside for them.

Riker gaped in shock. The mob raced past the peace officers, up the broad marble steps, between the tall black marble columns, and straight to the hospital's front door. They began to pound on the glass doors with their fists.

"Death to mixers!" they continued to shout. "Death to mixers! Death to mixers!"

Riker let one hand fall to his concealed phaser. If the crowd burst into the hospital and went on a killing spree, the three of them would have no choice but to reveal themselves and try to stop the rioters—without the help of the peace officers, if necessary. *If only we had real phasers,* he thought with frustration. A single hit on light stun might render a lightly built man unconscious for a few minutes, but burly men like so many of these— men with their adrenaline already pumped up— would hardly notice it.

Suddenly a forcefield crackled to life. It stretched across the whole front façade of the hospital . . . and slowly it began to extend outward, pushing all the attacking men and women away from the doors and windows, then down the steps toward the street. Riker let himself relax. It seemed the hospital had prepared for Father Veritas and his followers after all—and had a safe, nonviolent solution to the problem. He couldn't have come up with a better answer himself.

Relieved, he turned his attention back to the platform. Several people with old-fashioned megaphones had taken Brother Paul's place—and Brother Paul was nowhere to be seen now. *Spirited off to Purity League Headquarters, no doubt,* Riker thought with dismay. *If only I had a minute to talk to him.*

He squinted, but the floodlit glow that had surrounded Brother Paul was gone, making it difficult to see. Since the men now on the platform all wore shorter beards and plain clothes, in the semidarkness he didn't think he was seeing them well enough to be able to identify them again.

Shouting "A pure race is a good race!" and "Mixers must never be tolerated," they exhorted the audience to rise up and take back their planet. But the moment had passed; Brother Paul's magic no longer worked, at least not for these pedestrian rabble-rousers. The crowds began to disperse, streaming off down the five convergent streets in knots of ten or twenty at a time.

"Sir," Data said, "perhaps we should try to follow one of the groups."

Riker nodded. He had just been thinking the same thing. He turned slowly, looking at the crowd still around the podium.

The assembled people liked what they were hearing. Some cheered, while others continued to chant "Veritas!" over and over.

And just as suddenly as the riot had begun, the whole demonstration seemed to end. Men and women streamed away from the square, heading up the five streets that led away. The people with the megaphones hopped down and fled.

"Which way, Will?" Data asked.

Riker hesitated, turning slowly. Some of the rioters had begun to smash windows, throw stones, and try to overturn ground cars along the various streets. The peace officers had given up their posts and joined in.

But he had a feeling these people were, if not innocent, at least not clued in to the ringleaders. Cattle, easily manipulated, sent to do the Purity League's dirty work.

He made his decision: "This way." And he started up the street after the men with the megaphones.

Chapter Sixteen

AFTER HIS THIRD TANKARD of blood wine, Worf felt himself getting as plastered as the rest of his new-found Klingon friends. His tongue kept tripping over itself, but between bouts of song, fistfights, and bragging matches, he managed to piece together most of the details of what had brought Captain Krot and his men to this place.

Captain Krot had realized his ship would be caught on Archaria III as soon as the plague broke loose if he did not move quickly. Their cargo—fifty thousand tons of grain, destined for the qagh farms on Kra'togh IV—had already been delivered. They just had a few repairs to make to their warp drive.

"If we had left one day sooner," Krot said, "we

never would have known about the plague. Bah! Bad luck follows me."

After cunningly bribing the docking clerk in charge of their vessel, they'd lifted off. "Your life will be spared if you delete our departure record!" Krot had said. He burst out laughing when he tried to describe the clerk's horrified expression when faced with a mek'leth at his throat!

Unfortunately, their emergency warp-drive repairs had not held up. Due to primary warp-core failure, they had only gotten as far as orbit.

It was then that they picked up a transmission to the *Enterprise.* Immediately Krot ordered a landing on one of the moons . . . and they were fortunate enough to spot this old base. It already had two ships parked here—they figured they would wait out the plague while they made repairs.

"We did not know that Klingons ran the *Enterprise!*" Krot proclaimed. Worf silently congratulated himself on discretely returning his human away team to the Enterprise shortly after his first cup of blood wine. The captain raised his tankard. "To Klingons everywhere!"

"To Klingons!" Worf echoed.

The rest of Krot's crew began to chant, again, and Worf drained his blood wine in two long gulps.

The world swam fuzzily before dropping back into focus.

"What will you do now?" Worf asked. "The system is under quarantine. You may not leave."

"Why should I care about a human quarantine? This plague does not affect Klingons!"

"It is better to cooperate," Worf said sagely.

"Have another drink!" Krot passed him a tankard. "And tell me more about this great Captain Picard of yours! Perhaps he will listen to reason— or a mek'leth, eh?"

"You must meet him! He is a great leader. Do not pull a mek'leth on him, though, or I will have to kill you!"

"Just try!"

Worf struggled to his feet. He couldn't quite get them to work. *Too much blood wine,* he realized. *Maybe—maybe I have said enough.*

Krot was laughing.

That was the last thing he remembered.

Chapter Seventeen

AS THEY TRAILED THE MEN AND WOMEN responsible for organizing the rally at the hospital, Riker tried to get as close to them as he could without attracting their attention. Luckily they seemed too preoccupied . . . they never looked back to see if anyone was following. They simply assumed they were safe. *Amateurs*, Riker realized thankfully. *They really have no idea what they're doing, do they?*

Perhaps a hundred other rally-goers had taken this street away from the square. With all their talk and chatter—mixed in with more chanting and slogan-shouting—Riker had a hard time trying to eavesdrop on the people he was following.

He caught bits and pieces:

"*. . . mixers must be purged soon, or—*"

". . . save our families before the next plague—"

". . . across the bridge, you know—"

None of it made much sense, though a lot of it offered tantalizing hints. The next plague? What did they know about the virus?

He quickened his pace, closing the gap, straining to hear more.

They left the commercial part of the city, crossed a small bridge, and entered a residential area. Tall houses now surrounded them, pressing close to each other.

Unfortunately, they chose that moment to pause in front of one of the houses. He almost walked into them and had to step around and keep going to avoid attracting their attention. He cursed his luck, and caught another fragment of dialog:

". . . can't be trusted tonight. Maybe tomorrow, if—"

Then they all entered the house and the door slammed shut. He heard a deadbolt slam home. Just when it had started to get interesting! "So much for that—" he said.

He turned to Yar and Data. "Did you hear any more of what they were saying than I did?"

"I heard everything, sir," Data replied.

That's right—Data had far keener hearing than a human, as well as a photographic memory.

"Summarize," he said. "What did they say? I caught something about a second plague—are they planning to wipe out the Peladians next?"

"No, sir. They believe the Peladians are responsible for the first virus, and that a second one is coming to finish the job. It is supposed to wipe out all the humans on the planet."

Riker shook his head. "Then they don't know anything about it."

"Apparently not."

He had chosen the wrong group to follow.

He turned around and found the street deserted. "And we lost the rest of the rioters."

"Perhaps we should return to the hospital," Data suggested. "It might be possible to pick up Brother Paul's trail," Data suggested. "Someone might have seen which way he went."

"That's our best hope," Riker agreed. "Let's go!"

They set off at a jog, and fifteen minutes later they reached the hospital complex once more. Most of the people had left, but several hundred had stayed behind. They all stood around the bonfire, drinking, singing protest songs, and watching the flames. It seemed rather pathetic to Riker.

He searched the faces in the crowd but did not recognize anyone. *Another dead end,* he thought bitterly. This mission was not going well.

"Sir." Data pointed to the left, and Riker squinted into the darkness at several shapes moving along the hospital's wall behind the bushes. They moved like phantoms, keeping low to the ground.

"What are they doing?" he asked Data softly. "Your eyes are better than mine."

"They appear to be planting explosive charges. However, from the looks of the devices they are not powerful enough to do any real damage. The hospital's forcefield will protect it."

Riker sucked in a deep breath. "Terrorists . . . this is what we've been waiting for. Keep an eye on them—we're going to chase them all the way to Father Veritas if we have to!"

The shapes suddenly sprinted away from the hospital. A heartbeat later, a series of brilliant flashes and thunderous explosions sounded. Bushes flew and clods of dirt started to rain down. The people around the bonfire began to scream and run for cover.

"Now!" Riker shouted, sprinting. Data and Tasha Yar followed.

Together, they pounded up the street, gaining steadily on the terrorists. These men had a little more sense than the rally organizers—they kept glancing back, and clearly knew they were being followed.

At a five-way intersection, they split up. Riker picked the middle terrorist and kept chasing him. From behind, he heard sirens begin to ring. *Here comes the cavalry,* he thought, tucking down his head and speeding up his gait.

The man seemed to know he was about to be caught, since he abruptly stopped, turned, and raised his arm.

"Phaser!" Riker shouted. He dove to the side a heartbeat ahead of the beam of brilliant blue light that lashed out at him. He rolled to his feet and darted into an alley for cover.

The terrorist's weapon had been set on kill, he realized. Its beam played across the building behind him, blowing out part of the second-floor wall. Bits of bricks and mortar began to thud to the ground around him.

Riker scrambled for cover. The terrorist fired again, taking out a shop window. Flames leaped inside the building, and more alarms began to ring.

Riker ducked into an alley as a third shot nearly took off his head.

Panting, Riker pulled out his own phaser. He counted to three, leaned out, and fired. Years of target practice paid off—he caught the man square in the side.

But the terrorist seemed to shrug off the light stun setting. *I knew using local weapons was a mistake,* Riker thought. Next time he'd follow his instincts.

Raising his phaser, the terrorist fired at Riker again. Riker staggered back as the corner of the building exploded into debris. When he peeked out again, the man had taken off at a dead run.

Sirens wailed. Stepping out, Riker aimed his phaser and fired a second time. Once more he hit the mark—but once more the weak light-stun setting had little effect.

"Data! Yar!" he shouted.

"Here, sir!" came both voices.

That's one good thing. They're both still alive and safe.

After counting to ten, he peeked around the corner. Two buildings were on fire and a third had a hole in its second floor big enough to fly one of the *Enterprise*'s shuttles through. *The peace officers are not going to be happy,* he thought. *Not to mention the shopkeepers.*

"I think he's gone!" Riker shouted. "Join me in the alley!"

Yar dashed over, and a second later Data followed. Yar was disheveled and out of breath. Data looked a mess. Even by the dim, flickering light of the fires, Riker could see that Data's human make-up had been rubbed off along the whole left side of his face, revealing his golden skin. And one of his eyepieces had fallen out.

"I hear aircars closing in on our position," Data said. "I strongly suggest we move away from this alley, sir, before we are arrested."

"Right. We still have that terrorist to catch." He stepped out onto the street—but a couple of phaser shots lashed out at him. He wheeled back as bits of masonry blasted loose, peppering his face and hands. *That wasn't a stun setting,* he realized.

"I thought you said they didn't have kill settings enabled on their weapons!" he said to Yar, rubbing at the stinging little wounds. He was lucky they hadn't blinded him.

"That's only the civilians, sir. The peace officers have fully functioning phasers."

"Now you tell me!"

One of the burning buildings suddenly collapsed with a shower of sparks and an avalanche of duracrete slabs. Dust rose in a cloud—that would provide them with cover for a few minutes, he thought. They had to get out of here.

He glanced behind him, but the alley dead-ended. There was only one way out—the way they had come in.

"I don't think they saw you two," he said. "I'll draw their fire, then do an emergency beamout. Get past them and try to catch up with our terrorist friend."

"Where will we meet up?" Yar demanded.

"Back at the alley where we beamed in. Be there in one hour."

She gave a nod. "Got it."

Riker leaped from hiding with his phaser in hand, blasting at every figure he saw. *Just like target practice,* he thought.

Light stun certainly worked better at close range. One man fell, then another, then a third. Riker rolled, landed behind a pile of duracrete slabs and paused, listening. *Let them think I'm wounded.* He felt his heart pounding like a battering ram. *I'll catch them when they least expect it.*

On the count of ten, he leaped out again—but headed back the way he had come instead of making for the next natural hiding place. His tactic caught two more peace officers by surprise. They had been trying to sneak up behind him. A pair of perfectly executed shots took them down.

That's five. How many are there?

They would have caught him if he'd behaved like a sensible terrorist and tried to get away. *Too bad I'm neither sensible nor a terrorist. I'm not interested in getting away—at least, not on foot.*

He started counting again. *One more volley, then*

I'll have the Enterprise *beam me to safety,* he thought.

Licking his lips, he tensed to spring—but a sudden intense burst of phaser fire struck the building directly behind and above him. Bricks blasted outward, and he felt several strike his back, throwing him to the ground. Moaning in pain, he reached for his combadge—but it had come off. *Where?* His fingers scrabbled in the dirt and debris, searching.

"Riker to *Enterprise,*" he said urgently, hoping it had somehow activated. "Emergency beamout—"

Then something struck the back of his head, and he knew no more.

Chapter Eighteen

TASHA YAR RAN until she thought her lungs would burst, and she still saw no sign of the terrorist in black. He must have turned off somewhere. They must have lost him.

She drew to a halt. Data paused, looking back at her. "Tasha?"

"I have to rest," she panted. She put her hands on her knees and bent over, feeling sick and dizzy.

Since leaving Commander Riker, they hadn't had any luck. The peace officers had spotted them and given chase, and it seemed an alert had been raised. Everywhere they went, they spotted uniformed men in riot gear.

"This is not the place for a rest," Data said.

She nodded. "I know. But there's nothing I can do about it. I can't go any farther!"

A line of peace officers rounded the corner several blocks up. They wore helmets and carried heavy shields and phasers in their hands—and for Tasha Yar, it brought back a flood of terrible memories. As a fist of panic clutched her heart, she felt herself start to shake. *I'm not home. This isn't a rape gang. If things get bad, all we have to do is beam back to the* Enterprise.

"This way, Tasha," Data said urgently, grabbing her arm and pulling her up a narrow street.

Her legs felt like deadwood, but Yar forced them to move. Data had better eyesight than she did; he must have spotted something, she thought—some way of escape short of an emergency beamout.

At least this alley smelled better than the first; hulking shapes of discarded packing material and machinery blocked her way, but she darted around them.

Suddenly Data pulled her into a deeply recessed doorway. "Shh!" he said.

Behind them, she heard footsteps entering the alley. Bright lights swung up and down the length. *Great. We're trapped.*

"I have bad news," he told her in a soft voice.

"It can't get any worse!"

"This appears to be a dead end."

"What!" She turned and looked at him. "You've got to be kidding! I thought you knew where you were going!"

"It seemed the logical place to run."

She bit her lip, then turned and tried the door behind them. It had an old-style round knob, smooth and hard and cold. And, of course, it was locked. And, of course, a phaser set on stun wouldn't open it. *I should have insisted we bring live weapons,* she thought. *What was I thinking? Never again!*

"Data . . . can you force this door open?" she asked.

"That would be an illegal act," he said. "Federation code 44.1.6 clearly states—"

"Circumstances warrant it! *Open the door!*"

"Very well." He gripped the knob and turned it sharply. Metal inside the knob broke. Then he pushed, but the door still didn't move.

"It appears to be bolted from the inside."

"So push!"

Using the flat of his hand, Data gave the door a sharp jab perhaps twenty centimeters above the knob. The wood splintered.

Yar glanced toward the street. Lights continued to sweep the length of the alley. The peace officers were making their way through boxes fifteen meters away.

"Hurry!"

Data rammed his fist through the hole with a loud bang, and as she watched with growing fear, he felt around inside.

One of the peace officers shouted, "I think they're ahead of us!"

"Ah. A simple deadbolt," Data said.

He slid it aside, withdrew his arm, and pushed the door open. *Finally!* Yar ducked inside, and Data followed, closing the door with a slight squeak.

Pitch darkness surrounded her. She paused, listening to the pounding of her heart, waiting for cries of *"There they are!"* from the peace officers.

"Shall I brace the door closed in case they try to break it down?"

"With what?"

"There is sufficient lumber on the floor."

"Then do it!"

Outside, someone tried the doorknob.

"I am holding it," Data whispered. "They will not pass."

Something heavy—a pair of shoulders?—thumped against the wood. Evidently Data's strength convinced them that entry wasn't possible; they moved on, talking in low voices.

"How well can you see?" she asked.

"Well enough," said Data. "There is sufficient infrared radiation for me to navigate the warehouse."

She hesitated. "Don't take this the wrong way. But I want you to take my arm and lead me to another exit."

"I have a better idea, Tasha." Picking her up in his strong arms, he carried her on a twisting course through the length of the warehouse. At last he stopped and set her down.

"Where are we?"

"The other side of the warehouse. This door is marked 'Exit.' "

She heard him undo a couple of bolts, then he opened a heavy steel fire door half a centimeter. A blade of light fell inside—she blinked, then realized it wasn't that bright, just spillover from the street. They were looking out onto a small side street.

Tasha put her eye to the crack and peeked out. The peace officers had moved on, apparently. The street was deserted.

She opened the door and eased out. Pressed up against the building, she made her way to the main street at the front of the building, peeked around the corner, and gave a sigh of relief. She saw the peace officers' backs—they were moving up the street quickly.

Then she froze in place. Movement on a nearby rooftop had caught her eye. A sniper?

"Data," she whispered. "Get up here! Who is that?"

She pointed across and up twenty meters to the roof of another warehouse. A man stood silhouetted against the larger moon. He was gazing at the peace officers. And he held something dark in his hands. *A phaser?*

"I believe he is taking atmospheric samples," Data said. "The device he is holding is a Starfleet tricorder of the type used on planetary surveys. It collects data from monitoring stations."

That puzzled her. "What's he doing out at this hour? It has to be past midnight!"

"It is 1:07 A.M., according to the local clock. The man appears to be waiting for the peace officers to leave. His expression appears nervous."

Interesting. He's doing something illegal. She felt a rising suspicion. "Something isn't right here," she said.

"I agree. He does not appear to be wearing a Starfleet uniform. Nor do I recognize him as one of the *Enterprise*'s crew. He should not be carrying Starfleet equipment."

"I meant he doesn't belong on top of a warehouse in the middle of the night," Yar said. "He's up to something. He might be one of the terrorists."

"Unlikely," Data said. "His build does not match that of any of the three men we chased. However, I agree that his presence and actions do appear suspicious. What course of action do you suggest?"

"Simple. Let's question him."

"How?"

She drew her phaser and passed it to him. "You're the expert marksman. If you hit him with both our phasers, it should stun him, even at this distance. Then it's just a matter of picking him up and interrogating him."

"What if he has legitimate business?"

"Then we apologize and buy him a drink at the nearest bar."

"Very well." Data accepted her phaser with his left hand, then pulled out his own with his right.

He stepped forward, raised both arms, and fired both phasers simultaneously.

Both beams struck the man's chest. *Perfect shot!* Yar thought. Without a sound, he collapsed and lay still.

It took them five minutes to get across the street and up to the roof. A large and rather flashy aircar waited there with its door open and its powerful engines idling. Yar switched on its lights, and their glow lit up the whole rooftop.

"It would appear he landed here to watch the peace officers," Data said.

"Not with this tricorder." She picked it up and handed it to him. "What do you make of it?"

"Starfleet issue. A current model. It should not be in civilian hands."

"Then what was he doing with it?"

Data turned slowly. "There—that is the atmospheric monitoring station he must have been checking." He crossed to the small silver box and pulled it off the wall. When he flipped open the top, he read something inside. "As I expected, it is set to monitor particle content in the air."

"Do you mean dust?"

"Any particulate matter—dust, pollution, and pollen are three examples."

"How about . . . an airborne virus?"

"Like the plague virus?"

"Exactly."

"It would count that, too."

The man began to stir and moan. Tasha regarded him suspiciously. "I think we've just found the key to the puzzle," she said. "Keep him covered."

Crossing to where he lay, she began searching through his pockets. Not one but two phasers, a knife, and three sets of identification cards . . . all very interesting. One ID claimed he was a grain buyer, another an engineering-supply salesman, and the third a missionary priest. *A priest?* She knew they were fake; a grain-buying engineering-sales missionary-priest might conceivably exist, but each of the three IDs gave different names and home planets.

He stirred and moaned. *He'll be awake soon. Might as well get it over with.*

"Wake up!" she said, giving his shoulder a shake.

He opened his eyes suddenly and gasped. "What—where—"

"That's what I want to know," she said with an unkind smile. Phaser stuns left people disoriented; she meant to take advantage of it. "Who are you— really—and what can you tell me about this plague?"

"Let go of me!"

She released him. With Data standing there, he wouldn't get away.

"I work for the Archo City Hospital," he said, sitting up and rubbing his head. "What happened?"

"Uh-uh. Not with these ID cards, you don't. And you don't have a beard; you're no Archarian." She fanned the identification cards out in front of his face. "And I'll stake my job none of these is you. Care to try again?"

He climbed to his feet, brushed himself off, and adjusted his collar. An almost mocking smile came over his face. "Not this time."

Lights shimmered, and he began to disappear as a transporter beam energized around him.

"No you don't!" Yar cried.

She leaped into the beam with him—and the next thing she knew, they were standing on a single transporter pad in a small, nearly dark room—a spaceship?

She grabbed his shirt and flung him into the bulkhead. He hit with a bone-jarring crunch and an "oof" of pain.

"Give up," she said.

"You'll die!" he snarled and grabbed for something on the wall. *A phaser?*

She leaped forward and kicked him in the stomach, then gave him a chop to the back to the neck when he doubled over in pain. He collapsed, shuddered once, and didn't move.

"Computer—more light!" she called.

The room brightened. She turned slowly, taking stock of the situation . . . she was in a cramped little cabin stuffed to overflowing with equipment. And a lot of it looked like Starfleet property.

I've hit the jackpot, she thought. *If he isn't involved with the plague, I'm a Vulcan princess.*

Three huge metal cylinders, stamped with tiny

print, stood along the back wall. She crossed to examine one. The pressure gauge read 0.004. Whatever had been inside wasn't there now.

Turning, she looked at the racks of assault rifles, phasers, and other weapons covering the second wall, the one to which she had him pinned. Shivering, she realized how lucky she had been. *If he'd gotten one of those, I would be toast now.*

She folded back the collar of her shirt, revealing her combadge, and tapped it once. "Yar to *Enterprise*," she said.

"*Enterprise*. Habbib here," came an ensign's voice.

"Locate Commander Riker and Lieutenant Commander Data and beam them to these coordinates."

"Lieutenant Commander Data has been located . . . Commander Riker is not wearing his combadge, however."

That didn't sound like Riker. *He'll be all right,* she told herself. *He's a survivor. Like me.*

"Thanks," she said. "If you locate Commander Riker, let me know."

"Yes, Lieutenant. *Enterprise* out."

The shimmer of a transporter beam appeared next to her, and Data materialized an instant later. He turned slowly, looking around the cabin, then bent to examine the unconscious man.

"He is dead," Data announced.

"What! That's impossible!" She stared incredulously at his body. "I didn't hit him that hard!"

"Nevertheless, he *is* dead."

Quickly she bent and rolled him over. She got a whiff of something acrid—*pentium xolinate*. It was a Cardassian drug, invariably fast and fatal.

"Suicide," she said, frowning. "He took poison. He must have had it hidden in a tooth."

Data moved to the cylinders. "We need to analyze these," he said suddenly.

"Could they hold something biological?" she asked.

"Like a virus?" Data asked. "It is a possibility. Biological agents are usually seeded into the atmosphere of a planet at least half a kilometer above the surface, however, to allow a wide dispersal through wind currents."

"He had a transporter."

Data paused. "It is theoretically possible to beam compressed gasses; they would expand immediately upon transport. That might be a highly effective method of seeding an atmosphere."

That's how he did it, Yar thought. *I know that's how he did it!*

Data continued to examine the cylinders. "They are marked 'Agricultural Prions.' However, a label does not always adequately represent a container's true contents."

"The expression is 'Don't judge a book by its cover.'"

"I believe that is what I said."

"We have to get them up to the *Enterprise*." Frowning, she moved to the front of the ship and gazed out the viewport at a vast duracrete landing field. The morning twilight had just begun. In the thin gray predawn light, she saw dozens of larger starships surrounding their little ship. *We're in the Archo City Spaceport,* she thought.

"Let's fly her up to one of the shuttle bays," she said suddenly, sliding into the pilot's seat. "We can get a security team aboard and strip her down to her bulkheads, if necessary. Our friend there must be involved in the plague, somehow."

"That would seem a logical conclusion," Data said.

The ship's controls hadn't been locked or encrypted, Yar saw. With the hatches dogged, he must have considered his ship secure. He hadn't counted on her beaming aboard with him.

Powering up the impulse engines, she studied the layout of the controls. Basic operations appeared straightforward. She knew she wouldn't have any trouble flying this ship.

An intercom crackled: "This is Archo Spaceport Control. Power down your engines, *Paladium*. This planet is quarantined—you may not lift off."

"Negative, Control," Yar said. "This is Lieutenant Yar. I am bringing this vessel up for a rendezvous with the *Enterprise.*"

"Permission to lift off is expressly denied," the voice insisted. "Power down, *Paladium,* or we will be forced to take drastic action!"

She glanced at Data. "Drastic action? What are they capable of, putting us on report? They don't have any pursuit ships or missile batteries. This is an agricultural planet."

"I believe they are bluffing," Data said.

"That's all I need to know." Tasha Yar brought the engines to full life. A low but powerful vibration spread through the hull. She initiated the liftoff sequence.

"Paladium!" Control said. *"Power down! Now!"*

"Negative," she replied. "You have our flight plan. We'll see you in orbit."

She lifted off smoothly, and the landing field began to dwindle away below.

Next she tapped her combadge. "Yar to *Enterprise,"* she said.

"Enterprise. Habbib here."

"We are aboard a small starship called the *Paladium,"* she said. "We are bringing it up now. Slap a level-one forcefield around this ship as soon as we land in the shuttle bay."

"No containment field is necessary," Habbib said. "Restrictions on travel to and from the planet to the *Enterprise* have been lifted."

"Then we have a cure for the plague?" She felt a brief surge of elation.

"Negative, *Paladium.* The virus is on the *Enterprise* as well. We are now under the same quarantine restrictions as Archaria III."

Yar exchanged a look with Data. *How—* She shook her head. *Someone was sloppy,* she thought.

She said to Habbib, "I want a security detail standing by when we land. And alert sickbay. We may have the cause of the plague on board."

"Understood, *Paladium,*" Habbib said. "Security will be standing by. *Enterprise* out."

"That's it!" Control snarled over the intercom. *"We are fining your account one hundred thousand credits,* Paladium!"

"Go ahead," Yar replied. She severed the connection and accelerated toward the *Enterprise.*

Chapter Nineteen

THE ANNOYING BUZZ in the back of Will Riker's head slowly materialized into the murmur of voices. He opened one eye to the smallest of slits. *Big mistake.* Fireworks seemed to go off inside his skull, flares and starbursts and supernovas all mixed up together. He groaned despite himself and pressed his eye shut again. *Everything hurts.* Even breathing was a chore. He couldn't remember feeling this bad since his big second-year survival drop at the Academy. *A week alone on a jungle planet with only a knife, a compass, and my wits. Why did I ever elect to take Advanced Survival before I was really ready for it?* The raw elements—including a six-day hurricane to beat anything ever seen on Earth—had defeated him utterly when a tree blew over and pinned him down. He had lain there in the muck and mud, feeding the alien equivalent of giant leeches, for three days until rescuers arrived. He had counted himself lucky to survive.

This time, it had been a building.

At least I am *waking up,* he thought, trying to feel optimistic. There was a faint ringing sound in his ears just a few octaves below the chatter of voices. An outside noise? An inside noise? Hallucination? *Better hurt than dead.* That's what his instructor, Dr. Neelam, had told him when he limped in to give his oral report on his failure. *Kindly Dr. Neelam.* The image of his instructor's beaming face appeared in his mind, Dr. Neelam saying: "The sloppiest job I've ever seen, but you lived through it, Bill."

"I'm called Will now," he told Dr. Neelam.

"Hey, pal," a rough voice beside him said. "Ready to try sitting up?"

"Huh?" Riker opened both eyes, and after the world stopped moving, he managed to focus on the speaker—a man about his own age, tall and broad-shouldered, dressed all in shades of brown right down to a long dark shag of brown beard. He was grinning—a friendly grin, Riker decided after a minute's hesitation.

Archaria III. Away team. Right.

"The sleeper wakes!" the man went on. Offering his hand, he said, "Want me to help you sit up, pal? I hear your name is Will."

"Was I talking out loud?"

"Yep. Need a hand?"

"Uh . . . give me a minute. Where am I?"

"Some detention center. I'm not quite sure which one yet. Probably East Quadrant. That's where they nabbed us."

"Oh." Gingerly he felt his scalp. Assorted lumps, bumps, cuts, and abrasions—perhaps even a mild concussion, from the ringing in his ears. *I'll ask Dr. Neelam to look me over first thing. No, I mean Dr. Crusher.*

Wait. That was back on the ship. He paused, frowning. The *Enterprise.* Where was he? *Under a building. No. In a detention center.* He tried to focus on his newfound friend, the beaming man with the beard. What was the fellow's name? Had he said?

"Where—" he said again. *No, I already asked that.*

"Say, you are fuzzed out, aren't you? Dee-ten-shun Cen-ter. East Quadrant. They got a hundred and twelve of us in the roundup." The man gave a low chuckle and offered his hand. Riker took it, and the man pulled him to a sitting position.

That was a mistake. The world swirled like a whirlpool around him.

"You have a family name, Will?"

"Riker."

"Don't know 'em, sorry." He stuck out his hand again. "Mine is Clarence Darling."

"Clarence *Darling?*"

"Yes, sweetheart." Clarence rolled his eyes. "Old name. First settlers, so we're supposed to be proud. Nothing to do about it now."

At least Clarence had a sense of humor. Riker gave a low chuckle as he turned his head—not too quick!—to look around. Despite his caution, the room rolled like a ship on high seas, the floor rising up, the walls moving in. He tasted bile and gulped hastily. The ringing in his ears grew worse, louder and more shrill, a perfect bell tone had it come from a bell.

He pressed his eyes shut again. *I should have been a doctor. I could have healed myself.*

"Hope you don't mind," Darling said, "but I kind of appointed myself your watchdog. While you were unconscious, I mean. The pos picked you clean, but at least *our* side left you alone."

Pos? Oh . . . PO's—peace officers. He hadn't heard that slang term in years; it figured that it would still be circulating on a backwater planet like Archaria III. *Picked me clean . . . ?* Riker pulled himself up on his elbows—*Slowly! Don't rush it!*—and noticed his boots were missing. He still had his slightly fuzzy brown socks, though. They looked a little silly, and he wiggled his toes and took a perverse delight in noting *they* didn't hurt. They were the only thing in his whole body without their own private aches and pains.

Then more urgently he felt his pockets. *All gone. Phaser, combadge, everything.* He really had been cleaned out. Everything of any potential value had been removed. *Great. Humanity is supposed to be beyond racial prejudice, let alone petty thievery.*

"The pos roll everyone who comes in unconscious. Must be the Ferengi in them." Darling frowned suddenly. "You don't look so good all of a sudden. I think you need a doctor, Will. Better lie down till we can get out of here." He put one hand on Riker's chest and pushed him gently back onto the bench where he had been lying. "That's an order, soldier!"

Riker stiffened. *Soldier. Does he know I'm from the Federation? No, can't be, I'm not a soldier, anyway. Never mind that Bili used to call me that.* It had to be just a slang term of affection for a newfound friend, like "pal." *And I need a friend here. No combadge, no rescue. Dr. Neelam would approve. It's my survival test all over again.*

He focused his eyes on a water stain on the ceiling tiles directly overhead. The ringing in his head let up a little. The burble of voices rose around him. *What I wouldn't give for a minute of perfect silence. Or a doctor. Or a combadge—*

"I don't think we'll be here much longer," Darling said suddenly. "It's nearly dawn."

Riker felt something run down his cheek and

gave a little shudder. *Bugs.* He hated bugs. But when he touched the spot, his fingers came away wet. *Not bugs. Blood.* He stared at the crimson smear. *A doctor. I'd better call Dr. Crusher. Time for the cavalry to rescue me. So much for Billy-the-Kid Riker, boy hero.*

What would Captain Picard do? *The captain wouldn't split up or lose his combadge or let a building fall on his head.* This was going to make one hell of a bad report. One *hell* of a bad report. *At least Data and Yar got away.* Rescue? He could have laughed—they wouldn't even know where to look. He'd have to find them . . . if they hadn't already reported him missing to the *Enterprise.*

The alley . . . perhaps they would be waiting for him there.

He levered himself up on his elbows again. And just like before, the universe began to tilt alarmingly. He felt himself starting to slide off the world, almost as though gravity weren't working quite right here. But that was ridiculous, wasn't it?

With a "Mph!" he lay back down. "Do I get to make a call, or am I stuck here?" he asked Darling. He forced the words out slowly. "What's the, ah, protocol for being arrested these days?"

"You *are* new to this rabble-rousing stuff, aren't you?" Darling chuckled. "There are too many of us. The most they're going to do is charge us with misdemeanors, issue citations, and chuck us out on our ears. And they probably won't even bother with the citations because nobody's going to pay them. Most of the pos are members of the League anyway. If they weren't on duty, they'd all be with us in the streets. After all, we all want the same thing, right?"

"Yeah." He had definitely gotten the impression that the peace officers supported the League. Had it only been last night? It seemed an eternity away.

Riker took a deep breath, shuddering a bit at a new stabbing pain in his left shoulder. *What's the first thing you do after a disaster? Take inventory.* No boots, no possessions. Easy enough. He slowly flexed his muscles. *Focus,* he told himself. Fingers, hands, arms; feet, legs, neck, and spine. All extremities in place. Lots of small pains, a couple of larger cuts and abrasions on his hands where he had fallen. Plus the assorted injuries to his head and that stabbing pain in his shoulder. Bruised but not broken, by and large, he decided. *I'd give anything for those bells to stop ringing.* If only he could think clearly. *A plan. I need a plan. What would Dr. Neelam do? "Survival first," he always said in class. "Worry about the civilized niceties later."*

Darling said, "So, spill the details. What happened to you, Will?"

"I got in a firefight with the pos and a building fell on me." He turned his head to look around the room more carefully. This time at least it stayed on an even keel. "Rather, the pos blasted it down on top of me."

"They used phasers set on high?" Darling gave a low whistle. "First I've heard of them using deadly force against us! Well, almost deadly force. You must have really gotten them angry."

"Afraid so. It was my own damn fault. We didn't want to be arrested and stunned two of them."

"Ever been picked up before?"

"No."

"I thought so. I tried to fight it my first time, too—and got my skull bashed with a billy for my troubles. This is my fifth time. Peaceful cooperation, that's the only way, once they've made the pinch."

"But what about . . ." He lost his train of thought for an instant and floundered. "You know?"

Darling seemed to pick up on it. "If you're in here with us, that means they didn't write you up. You're just another drunk-and-disorderly Leaguer they arrested for disturbing the peace. And with things the way they are . . . they don't have enough prisons to hold us all, even if they wanted to." He shrugged. "They can't lock up half the planet, after all!"

"The human half, you mean."

Darling grinned wolfishly. "The human *majority.*"

For a second Riker saw the true nature of the League in his rescuer's eyes. *Not a friend.* It was insidious, these racist beliefs. And yet he knew he needed Darling—needed the decent human inside him who would go out of his way to help a stranger.

Doors on the far side of the room banged open, and a short man in a black uniform strolled in, frowning. Unlike the others, he was clean-shaven and there was something odd about the shape of his skull . . . too elongated, too pointy on top.

Hisses, boos, and jeering catcalls greeted him. "Mixer!" Riker heard Darling snarl under his breath. So that was it—this was a Peladian.

"Listen up!" the Peladian peace officer said in a loud voice. He thumped the data padd he held with one slender finger. "All prisoners are being released on their own recognizance. Take advantage of this little learning experience and stay indoors tonight. The governor has declared a curfew, and anyone caught on the streets after dark will face the full force of the law!"

Darling chuckled. So did most of the others in the room. Riker looked around in bewilderment. Were they insane as well as predjudiced?

"What's so funny?" he finally whispered.

"That's the same speech he's given every morning for the last week!" Darling replied.

The smooth-cheeked officer glared until the laughter died down. "That's better," he finally said. "Now, form a line and make your way outside in an orderly manner. If you cooperate, you'll be home for breakfast."

Turning, he stalked out the door with the data padd slapping against his thigh. More mocking laughter trailed him, and jeering cries of, "Get off the planet, mixer!"

"Damn arrogant bastard," Darling snarled under his breath. "Thinks he's better than us!"

Riker held his tongue, but couldn't stop the thought: *He* is *better than all of you.* Cordial as Darling seemed, the underpinnings of his Purity League beliefs left no doubt about his true nature: xenophobe, human-supremacist, and violent-terrorist. *I must not forget that,* Riker told himself. *He thinks I'm one of them. That's the only reason he's behaving so well toward me.*

Chapter Twenty

WORF WOKE SLOWLY and groaned. *My head!* If felt like a split melon. Sitting up, he looked blearily around the room.

Klingons lay sprawled everywhere around him, snoring. Krot—Skall—Karqq—all the others . . .

It was the blood wine, he thought with growing horror. He had forgotten to check in with the *Enterprise* and make his report. He knew a human captain wouldn't kill him for such an oversight, but he felt he deserved execution.

He had lost track of his mission. He had neglected his duty. . . .

Never again, he thought. Even though he had been exposed to the plague virus and could not return to the *Enterprise,* he should have made his report. They could have been depending on him.

Struggling to his feet, he staggered a bit as his center of balance shifted. He searched for his lost helmet and finally spotted it in the corner, where Krot had flung it. Picking it up, he fitted it back on his head. Luckily the comm unit still worked. He clicked it on with his chin.

"Worf to *Enterprise,*" he said.

"*Enterprise,* Habbib here," came the reply.

"I wish to make a report," he said. "I have been exposed to the plague virus and will be remaining on this moon until a cure is found."

"Negative, sir," came the reply. "The whole ship has been exposed to the plague virus. There is no longer a quarantine situation. Captain Picard left orders for you to be transported back the minute you report in."

Worf frowned. *That is not good news,* he thought. Something terrible must have happened aboard ship—a medical disaster—for the disease to be loose on board.

"Energize," he said.

He had a very bad feeling inside.

Dr. Crusher rubbed bleary, burning eyes. *Sixteen cases,* she thought. Between the *Enterprise* and the *Constitution,* they now had *sixteen* confirmed cases of the plague. *This is a nightmare.*

The medical teams of both ships had combined aboard the *Enterprise.* And they still weren't making any progress.

And Dr. Tang, whenever they consulted him,

seemed more depressed than ever. He continued to recommend quarantining the planet forever.

We need luck. And inspiration, Dr. Crusher thought. *We're missing something . . . something obvious.*

Not for the first time, she went back to the very core of the problem. *We have a virus that can squeeze through a level-1 containment field. How?* She studied its diagram on the monitor. *What are the possibilities?*

Teleportation? *Impossible!*

Changing its shape to something smaller? *Possible?* They had seen no sign of any metamorphic properties, however, and they had been watching live samples for hours. *Not likely,* she finally decided. *It's a form of Rhulian flu. It doesn't change shape.*

What else? *It needs a Trojan horse,* she thought. *Some way to sneak through a containment field without being caught or identified.* But it couldn't do that in its present form. It would have to be broken down and reassembled.

It's modular! Suddenly she had a horrible vision of how it might work. *Two or five or ten smaller parts, all coming together to form a virus . . . airborne miniparticles, drifting in the air until they meet up, then uniting to become the plague virus!*

She had never heard of any organism working in such a manner. But that didn't mean it wasn't possible. The added hooks on the NXA protein strands—those could be assembly instructions.

But it would have to be alive in its component parts, too. *What's alive but smaller than a virus?*

Nanotechnology? No, it couldn't possibly be mechanical in origin. Noroids? Sondarian frets? Prions? It could be any of those—or any of several dozen other obscure but normally innocuous life forms. *Things we don't screen out with biofilters because they're harmless,* she thought. *Things small enough to slip through a level-1 containment field.*

"Computer," she said. "Begin a new analysis of blood sample 76-B." That was the most recent specimen drawn from Deanna Troi. "Find and catalog every life form and ever matter particle smaller than a virus."

The computer spoke. *"There are an estimated two hundred thousand subviral particles. Analysis will take approximately forty-one minutes."*

Dr. Crusher sighed. More delays. But she didn't see any alternatives. They certainly weren't making any progress with standard techniques or antiviral drugs.

"Begin analysis," she said. This looked like another two-cup problem.

She headed for the replicator and made her first cup of tea. Just as she was about to settle down to wait out the computer report, Captain Picard and Captain van Osterlich strode into sickbay. Behind them, waiting in the hall, she saw half a dozen security officers.

She stood. "What's happened?" she asked.

"Yar and Data are on their way up," Picard said.

"They have stolen a starship. They claim it belongs to the man responsible for setting the plague loose on Archaria III."

Dr. Crusher felt her breath catch in her throat. *This could be the break we need,* she thought.

"What's on board?" she demanded. "Are there any cultures or samples . . . or a cure?"

"They weren't specific—but they have something they want analyzed immediately in xenobiology."

"Let's go," she said, grabbing a medical tricorder.

Yar piloted the *Paladium* into the *Enterprise*'s shuttle bay 2, then set the little ship down. After she had powered down the impulse engines, she unsealed the hatches, rose, and hurried into the main compartment.

Data had been busy taking down weapons, she saw. She whistled at the rack of ten Federation heavy assault phaser rifles he had uncovered.

"I haven't seen any of these since the war with Cardassia," she said, taking one down and turning it over in her hands.

"They are probably war surplus," he said. "This particular model was decommissioned seven years ago."

She turned hers over and examined the handle. The serial number had been neatly and methodically burned off with a phaser. No way to trace it back to whoever legally bought or sold it last. *Just another sign our unknown friend was up to no good,* she thought.

She put the phaser back into the rack, then glanced down at the man who had committed suicide rather than get caught. Everything seemed to point to his involvement in something big. And yet she saw no sign of anything to do with the virus . . . except those cylinders.

"Status report!" Captain Picard called, as he led Dr. Crusher and half-a-dozen others aboard.

Yar filled him in while Dr. Crusher hurried to the cylinders and began taking tricorder scans.

"This is it!" Crusher announced, and excitement made her voice crack. "These cylinders contain the three different elements that make up the plague virus! I want them beamed to xenobiology—we've got to start taking them apart to see how these prions work."

"Prions?" Captain Picard asked, looking puzzled.

"Yes—I figured it out in sickbay this morning. The virus is a composite organism. It consists of three prions. When they come together, they interlock, rewrite each other's RNA, and a virus cell is born. Individually the prions are harmless. We have hundreds of different ones in our bodies, and they don't do anything. Our transporter doesn't filter them out, and they are small enough when airborne to pass through a level-one containment field!"

"And that's how it got loose on my ship," Picard said, nodding. "It makes sense."

Data said, "We believe our suspect beamed the prions directly over the city, seeding the air. That's how it managed to disperse so quickly."

"I've got to get back to sickbay," Dr. Crusher said. "This is the best development we could have had. I know we'll have a cure soon."

Chapter Twenty-one

THEIR RELEASE WENT BETTER than Riker could have hoped. Darling spotted a couple more of his League pals and drafted them into helping get Riker out the door. They were burly, bearded men, strong as oxen, and when they draped Riker's arms across their shoulders for support, his feet barely touched the ground.

Darling signed all their names in an arrest record book, and five seconds later they were out on the street. The morning thoroughfares bustled with activity, and Riker sensed at once that something had happened—something big. An almost electric undercurrent ran through everyone in sight.

Darling grabbed a bearded man and demanded, "What happened? What's all the excitement?"

"Haven't you heard? They caught the man re-

219

sponsible for the plague! And Starfleet says they'll have a cure for it by nightfall!"

"Who was responsible?" Riker demanded.

"Some crazy off-worlder! Can you believe it? He wasn't even one of *us!*"

Pulling away, the man hurried down the street.

So much for the Purity League theory, Riker thought. He exchanged a glance with Darling. *I've spent the night chasing phantom terrorists, having buildings fall on my head, and getting locked up with racist crackpots—for nothing!*

"Well," Darling said, "that's quite a development. It *wasn't* the Peladians after all."

The man holding Riker's right arm let go. "You take him!" he said to Darling. "I have to get home—I want to see the news!"

"Me, too!" said Darling's other friend. He ducked out from under Riker's other arm and sprinted up the street.

Riker wobbled a bit, but Darling steadied him. "Hey, I'll still look out for you, pal," Darling said. "I've come this far. I'll see you safely home."

"If you can get me to a comm station," Riker said, "I'll call for transportation."

"Easily done!" Turning, Darling pointed to a public comm unit on the corner across from them. "Come on!"

He helped Riker hobble across the street, then stood watching while Riker activated the unit.

"This is William Riker," he said to the computer. "I need to talk to the duty officer aboard the *Starship Enterprise.*"

Darling gaped at him. "The *Enterprise?* Are you crazy? What do you want with Starfleet scum?"

"Just a second and I'll show you," Riker said.

In ten seconds Geordi La Forge appeared on the screen.

"What happened, sir?" La Forge said. "You look terrible. We've had half the peace officers in the city searching for you since midnight!"

"The peace officers arrested me," Riker said. "It's a long story. I need transportation to sickbay . . . I think I have a mild concussion . . . and maybe a couple of cracked bones."

"Right," La Forge said. "Stay there, sir. I'll trace the comm signal back to your location."

"Thanks." Riker turned to Darling, who was staring at him incredulously.

"You—you *lied* to me!" Darling said.

"No I didn't," Riker said. He grinned. "You made a lot of assumptions about me based on my appearance. Think about it the next time you see a mixer . . . or a Peladian!"

He hated to go out with a lecture, but somehow it seemed fitting. Darling certainly needed his myopic racist worldview expanded.

A transporter beam began to shimmer around him.

"People aren't always what they seem . . . and if you look, you'll find new friends in the *oddest* places!"

Chapter Twenty-two

"THIS IS HOW the virus works," Dr. Crusher said to the assembled senior officers of the *Enterprise* and the *Constitution*. The meeting room fell silent.

"The virus begins life as three different prions." A computer simulation showed the three different microorganisms. "Separately these prions are harmless. But when they meet up—in the air or in a human body—they join together to form a more complex organism . . . a multiprion."

The holographic projection showed all three prions integrating themselves into one larger cell.

"Their protein strands hook together, and a new multiprion is born. Its first task is to rewrite its own RNA. In effect, it turns itself into a virus cell. Now, imagine it happening with thousands of prions at once and you'll see how quickly people can become infected."

Captain Picard stepped forward. "Thanks to Dr. Spencer, Dr. Tang, and Dr. Crusher, we now have a cure—a fourth prion, one we designed ourselves. We have already begun seeding Archaria III's atmosphere with it. This fourth prion hunts for the other three, attaches itself to them, and disables the multiprion genetic codes. In short, they are turned back into harmless prions once more."

"Sir, who is responsible?" Geordi La Forge asked.

"Good question." Picard cleared his throat. "Officially, Starfleet and the planetary governor are assigning blame to the Purity League. That organization has been officially outlawed and disbanded, so some good has come out of this disaster."

"And unofficially?" Worf asked.

Van Osterlich rose. "Unofficially . . . we don't know. The one suspect we have is dead, and he doesn't seem to exist in any official Starfleet databases. His identity cards are fake. His starship's registration is fake. Nothing aboard his ship has a serial number or identification mark of any kind. He is simply a blank—officially, he doesn't exist. Whether he worked for himself or someone else is still open to conjecture. However, I think it's safe to say that this is the work of some outside party with significant resources . . . an organization that took advantage of the Purity League's racist attitudes to test a new type of weapon."

"The big question is motive," Captain Picard said. He looked from face to face, and his expression grew even more serious. "It can't be racial purity. It can't be the Purity Leage. In fact, Starfleet has only been able to come up with one possible motive. . . . *Practice.*"

In sickbay, William Riker lay on a biobed next to Deanna Troi, resting and listening to the almost jubilant hubbub around them. *They have their cure. Everything is going to work out.* He smiled.

"A penny for your thoughts," Deanna said.

He turned his head to face her. "You look terrible," he said. It was the first thing that popped into his mind. The white blisters that had covered her face were gone, but she still had a deathly white pallor.

"So do you, Bill. I'm just happy to be alive."

He chuckled. "You know I go by 'Will' these days, don't you."

"Yes . . . I wondered if you were going to tell me. Don't you feel comfortable enough with me to just talk anymore?"

He reached out his hand and took hers, then gave it a soft squeeze. "Of course I do, Deanna. Let down your guard. Listen to my emotions. You know how I truly feel."

She smiled. "You're naughty!"

He laughed. "You don't have to be an empath to sense *that!*"

Epilogue

THE GENERAL SAT in the command seat aboard his palatial ship, hugging his knees and gently rocking back and forth. *No, no, no!* he thought. All the news today was bad. *Solomon dead. The plague cured. Archaria III on the verge of racial peace for the first time in generations.* The Federation had turned disaster into triumph.

He snarled. He wanted to smash something. *Anything.*

Solomon had failed him. His scientists, whose best genetic weapon fizzled when put to the test, had failed him. *All this time, all this money. And for nothing!*

No, not for nothing. *It's a learning experience.* The speed with which the Federation had acted to contain his plague was commendable. Clearly his people would have to modify the disease further.

Two days, he thought. *It only took them two days!*

Pocket Books
Proudly Presents

Double Helix #2

VECTORS

Dean Wesley Smith
& Kristine Kathryn Rusch

Available Now from Pocket Books

Turn the page for a preview of
Vectors. . . .

TEROK NOR. Its name was as dark as its corridors. He actually found himself seeking the light, but carefully. Oh, so carefully. Sometimes his cloak malfunctioned, and he was seen. Partially, like a heat shimmer across desert sand, or an electronic memory buried in an old computer. But he was seen.

He didn't dare make that mistake here. The General didn't tolerate mistakes from his agents.

He stood in the shadows just to the left of the main entrance to a place called Quark's Bar. The area the Ferengi bartender had called the Promenade lay before him, turning away to the right, bending with the shape of the station design. The walls were gray, the floors gray, everything was gray. The Cardassians made no effort to decorate this place. Even the bar seemed dismal.

He shuddered and drew his cape around his body. He was glad he wouldn't have to stay here too long. This Terok Nor reminded him of his prison cell. He had lost too many years of his life there. He had spent too much time staring at gray metal walls, dreaming of escape. The metal walls, the ringing sound of boots against hard surfaces, the stench of fear—impossible to hide, even though the Cardassians kept their Bajoran prisoners separate from the rest of the population—permeated the place. If he shut his eyes, his other senses would find nothing to distinguish Terok Nor from that hideous cell, from that prison he finally left. The prison had changed him—made him bitter, made him wiser, made him more careful.

Oh, so careful.

Two Cardassian guards walked the wide passage. Their gray skin matched the depressing decor. The only thing that seemed wrong to him was the heat. By rights this station should have been as cold as its walls, but it wasn't. The heat was thick and nearly unbearable. He didn't know how anyone could stand being here for long. The heat also accentuated the smells: the processed air, the unwashed bodies, the Rokassa juice wafting out from the bar. The sensations were almost too much for him.

He reminded himself that Terok Nor was the perfect testing ground. Two races, living in close proximity, with others coming and going. Their petty differences didn't matter. That one race kept the other prisoner, that one made the other labor in uridium processing were merely details. The important factor was much larger.

Terok Nor was the perfect testing ground for the General. A closed system, for the most part. But anyone entering the system—or departing the system—would leave a record. A trail he could follow, should he so choose.

He didn't choose at the moment.

Now, he was most interested in Terok Nor itself.

To his right in the bar, crowds of uridium freighter pilots and crews shouted and laughed, the sounds echoing off the high ceilings. A few moments before, he'd been in there sitting at the bar, watching.

Waiting.

Trying to stay cool and block out the uridium smell with the odor of one of the pilots' Gamzian wine. But it hadn't helped, and besides, he couldn't see that well or hear that clearly with his cloak on.

A clang from the far end of the Promenade caught his attention. One of the Cardassian guards had dropped his phaser pistol, then grabbed the wall as if for support. The other guard bent over him, then glanced from side to side, as if worried that a Bajoran might see and take advantage.

He was too far away to hear their words. The first guard shrugged the other off. The second guard picked up the pistol and spoke into his communicator. Two guards who had apparently been patrolling just out of his line of sight ran toward the far end of the Promenade.

The first guard put an arm around the second, who again shrugged him off. The second tried to stand, and nearly collapsed. The first guard supported him, and together they walked along the walls, keeping as far out of sight as possible.

He felt excitement flash through him, and he tamped it down. He couldn't let his emotions interfere with his observations. This might be nothing. It was a bit early to see results. He hadn't expected anything so soon.

The guards passed him. He had to press himself against the gray metal so that they wouldn't brush him. They weren't conversing, although he wished they would. He wanted to know exactly what had happened.

He needed to know.

He had moved to follow the guards, but the Promenade gave him no cover. So he remained in the shadows.

He would wait here, in the heat and the stench, just as he had done in his cell. He was good at waiting, especially when he knew it would end. And it would end.

Soon he would get his answer.

STAR TREK®

Strange New Worlds III
Contest Rules

1) ENTRY REQUIREMENTS:

No purchase necessary to enter. Enter by submitting your story as specified below.

2) CONTEST ELIGIBILITY:

This contest is open to nonprofessional writers who are legal residents of the United States and Canada (excluding Quebec) over the age of 18. Entrant must not have published any more than two short stories on a professional basis or in paid professional venues. Employees (or relatives of employees living in the same household) of Pocket Books, VIACOM, or any of its affiliates are not eligible. This contest is void in Puerto Rico and wherever prohibited by law.

3) FORMAT:

Entries should be no more than 7,500 words long and must not have been previously published. They must be typed or printed by word processor, double spaced, on one side of noncorrasable paper. Do not justify right-side margins. The author's name, address, and phone number must appear on the first page of the entry. The author's name, the story title, and the page number should appear on every page. No electronic or disk submissions will be accepted. All entries must be original and the sole work of the Entrant and the sole property of the Entrant.

4) ADDRESS:

Each entry must be mailed to: STRANGE NEW WORLDS, *Star Trek* Department, Pocket Books, 1230 Sixth Avenue, New York, NY 10020.

Each entry must be submitted only once. Please retain a copy of your submission. You may submit more than one story, but each submission must be mailed separately. Enclose a self-addressed, stamped envelope if you wish your entry returned. Entries must be received by October 1st, 1999. Not responsible for lost, late, stolen, postage due, or misdirected mail.

5) PRIZES:

One Grand Prize winner will receive:

Simon and Schuster's *Star Trek: Strange New Worlds III* Publishing Contract for Publication of Winning Entry in our *Strange New Worlds III* Anthology with a bonus advance of One Thousand Dollars ($1,000.00) above the Anthology word rate of 10 cents a word.

One Second Prize winner will receive:

Simon and Schuster's *Star Trek: Strange New Worlds III* Publishing Contract for Publication of Winning Entry in our *Strange New Worlds III* Anthology with a bonus advance of Six Hundred Dollars ($600.00) above the Anthology word rate of 10 cents a word.

Contest Rules

One Third Prize winner will receive:

Simon and Schuster's *Star Trek: Strange New Worlds III* Publishing Contract for Publication of Winning Entry in our *Strange New Worlds III* Anthology with a bonus advance of Four Hundred Dollars ($400.00) above the Anthology word rate of 10 cents a word.

All Honorable Mention winners will receive:

Simon and Schuster's *Star Trek: Strange New Worlds III* Publishing Contract for Publication of Winning Entry in the *Strange New Worlds III* Anthology and payment at the Anthology word rate of 10 cents a word.

There will be no more than twenty (20) Honorable Mention winners. No contestant can win more than one prize.

Each Prize Winner will also be entitled to a share of royalties on the *Strange New Worlds III* Anthology as specified in Simon and Schuster's *Star Trek: Strange New Worlds III* Publishing Contract.

6) JUDGING:

Submissions will be judged on the basis of writing ability and the originality of the story, which can be set in any of the *Star Trek* time frames and may feature any one or more of the *Star Trek* characters. The judges shall include the editor of the Anthology, one employee of Pocket Books, and one employee of VIACOM Consumer Products. The decisions of the judges shall be final. All prizes will be awarded provided a sufficient number of entries are received that meet the minimum criteria established by the judges.

7) NOTIFICATION:

The winners will be notified by mail or phone. The winners who win a publishing contract must sign the publishing contract in order to be awarded the prize. All federal, local, and state taxes are the responsibility of the winner. A list of the winners will be available after January 1st, 2000, on the Pocket Books *Star Trek* Books website, www.simonsays.com/startrek/, or the names of the winners can be obtained after January 1st, 2000, by sending a self-addressed, stamped envelope and a request for the list of winners to WINNERS' LIST, STRANGE NEW WORLDS III, *Star Trek* Department, Pocket Books, 1230 Sixth Avenue, New York, NY 10020.

8) STORY DISQUALIFICATIONS:

Certain types of stories will be disqualified from consideration:

a) Any story focusing on explicit sexual activity or graphic depictions of violence or sadism.

b) Any story that focuses on characters that are not past or present *Star Trek* regulars or familiar *Star Trek* guest characters.

c) Stories that deal with the previously unestablished death of a *Star Trek* character, or that establish major facts about or make major changes in the life of a major character, for instance a story that establishes a long-lost sibling or reveals the hidden passion two characters feel for each other.

d) Stories that are based around common clichés, such as "hurt/comfort" where a character is injured and lovingly cared for, or "Mary Sue" stories where a new character comes on the ship and outdoes the crew.

9) PUBLICITY:

Each Winner grants to Pocket Books the right to use his or her name, likeness, and entry for any advertising, promotion, and publicity purposes without further compensation to or permission from such winner, except where prohibited by law.

10) LEGAL STUFF:

All entries become the property of Pocket Books and of Paramount Pictures, the sole and exclusive owner of the *Star Trek* property and elements thereof. Entries will be returned only if they are accompanied by a self-addressed, stamped envelope. Contest void where prohibited by law.

Look for STAR TREK Fiction from Pocket Books

Star Trek®: The Original Series

Star Trek: The Next Generation®

Star Trek: Deep Space Nine®

Star Trek®: Voyager™

Flashback • Diane Carey
Pathways • Jeri Taylor
Mosaic • Jeri Taylor

#1 *Caretaker* • L. A. Graf
#2 *The Escape* • Dean W. Smith & Kristine K. Rusch
#3 *Ragnarok* • Nathan Archer
#4 *Violations* • Susan Wright
#5 *Incident at Arbuk* • John Gregory Betancourt
#6 *The Murdered Sun* • Christie Golden
#7 *Ghost of a Chance* • Mark A. Garland & Charles G. McGraw
#8 *Cybersong* • S. N. Lewitt
#9 *Invasion #4: The Final Fury* • Dafydd ab Hugh
#10 *Bless the Beasts* • Karen Haber
#11 *The Garden* • Melissa Scott
#12 *Chrysalis* • David Niall Wilson
#13 *The Black Shore* • Greg Cox
#14 *Marooned* • Christie Golden
#15 *Echoes* • Dean W. Smith & Kristine K. Rusch
#16 *Seven of Nine* • Christie Golden
#17 *Death of a Neutron Star* • Eric Kotani
#18 *Battle Lines* • Dave Galanter & Greg Brodeur

Star Trek®: New Frontier

#1 *House of Cards* • Peter David
#2 *Into the Void* • Peter David
#3 *The Two-Front War* • Peter David
#4 *End Game* • Peter David
#5 *Martyr* • Peter David
#6 *Fire on High* • Peter David

Star Trek®: Day of Honor

Book One: *Ancient Blood* • Diane Carey
Book Two: *Armageddon Sky* • L. A. Graf
Book Three: *Her Klingon Soul* • Michael Jan Friedman
Book Four: *Treaty's Law* • Dean W. Smith & Kristine K.
    Rusch
The Television Episode • Michael Jan Friedman

Star Trek®: The Captain's Table

Book One: *War Dragons* • L. A. Graf
Book Two: *Dujonian's Hoard* • Michael Jan Friedman
Book Three: *The Mist* • Dean W. Smith & Kristine K. Rusch
Book Four: *Fire Ship* • Diane Carey
Book Five: *Once Burned* • Peter David
Book Six: *Where Sea Meets Sky* • Jerry Oltion

Star Trek®: The Dominion War

Book 1: *Behind Enemy Lines* • John Vornholt
Book 2: *Call to Arms . . .* • Diane Carey
Book 3: *Tunnel Through the Stars* • John Vornholt
Book 4: *. . . Sacrifice of Angels* • Diane Carey

Star Trek®: My Brother's Keeper

Book One: *Republic* • Michael Jan Friedman
Book Two: *Constitution* • Michael Jan Friedman
Book Three: *Enterprise* • Michael Jan Friedman

1252.01